Memories of Light

Michael Metzler Jr.

ISBN: 9798652760427

Cover art: Renee Metzler
Cover Design: Susannah Metzler

"It was quite an ocean, with the irregular shores of earth, but desert and frightfully wild in appearance…"

— Jules Verne, *Journey to the Centre of the Earth*

Memories of Light

PART I

The Middle Part

Memories of Light

1. The Move

I used to enjoy attending public school. That is, I used to enjoy it until I turned 14, launched myself into a regrettable 8th grade *and* switched schools at the start of the new school year. Yes, a lot of things happened then. Let me start with the first.

Firstly, I had just exited from a happy year of 13 where being a teen was the new cool thing, and entered into a terrible year of 14 in which you are just realizing how awkward teens are supposed to be and remember what you're supposed to act like as a teen in society. Second, I graduated into 8th grade, which wasn't very much of a consequence, since pretty much everyone in my family had predicted it would happen, despite the ample supply of evidence which suggested otherwise. Third, to make matters worse, my family decided to move from our friendly country-home, our friendly country school, and our friendly country neighborhood, and into an unknown city of a different state, far, far away. That's right. A stale and icy grey city. One of those lifeless ones that you see on TV where you can't see any humans, but just steel beams and opaque glass windows and featureless buildings.

Of all places, we moved there. And with that change came a different school. My dad and mom knew that my sister and I would just *love* it, so of course they were absolutely wrong. Even before laying eyes on the school, no, even before we *moved* I knew this new life boded ill for my future, and I hadn't changed my mind up till now.

We moved into our new apartment on one of those bleak featureless buildings I had previously mentioned, on a blustery winter day. Shortly after hauling our parched belongings into these smaller living quarters, we tried to accommodate ourselves to this new experience in the city.

My dad had enjoyed his job in the country, but when his position was disbanded, it soon became necessary that our whole family move to this particular location in order to maintain our monetary standard of living. How fateful was it that we happened to find ourselves in a land quite the opposite of that of our previous lives! The apartment was considerably smaller than our country home, *and* at the same time slightly more expensive. But apparently one pays to live as humanity at its finest — or most condensed — as I fondly thought of it at the time. One odd thing about our location was that we had no front or back yard, and nothing to officially call a front door as one might call it in the country lifestyle. Also, in order to enter our home, we had to cross a dim parking lot, go up a slow and dim-witted elevator, traverse across a corridor, and finally find ourselves at our door, six stories above ground floor.

And another thing: It frightened me when I crossed to the ground floor and was immediately confronted with a busy street, with a terrifying number of bright yellow blurs that would fly past—evidence of the number of taxis used. Such vehicles I had never witnessed before, though I knew what they were and how they were used. That is, my mom explained them to me when we arrived. I swear I wouldn't know what to do unless my mom had shown me everything. As I looked towards the dim figures of the looming skyscrapers, I can still remember her hand on my shoulder as she told me all about people in cities, how they spent their days making money in those offices, looking out towards us from their office cubicles, wishing they had a nice apartment like the one we had. She told me that I would like it here, and that she would always be here when I came home from school, and she could read to me until I fell asleep. And I believed her, almost. I had no choice but to believe her, believe that my life was worth living despite all the things that seemed to make it unbearable.

Unpacking our things into our apartment was a rather bewildering and disappointing job, since the more we unpacked, the more we came to the conclusion that we had hardly enough space. We barely fit our enormous grandfather clock in the entrance way, and barely fit the extra fridge and grand piano in the living room, and had to resort to mere cushions rather than a full-on antique couch to fill in the extra space. So when we guaranteed a place for our 75-inch TV, my younger sister was immediately gratified and earnestly applied herself to the task of searching through our many boxes, trying to find her Hello Kitty DVDs. After everything was set up, however, my fears had subsided considerably as I gradually took in the fact that our apartment would fit everything...barely. We settled in and everything seemed fine. That was until I remembered that I was attending a different school.

Its name was Lewis City Middle School.

I remember starkly in my mind the first time I set my eyes upon the signage. How could one forget? It was a large, grey one, prominent above the muted clay-like dirt and the black asphalt road. Its masonry was worn, and the words **Lewis City** were styled in cursive, while the words *Middle School* underneath were graven deeper, in a more modest design. I blinked at the cold stone features of the complex looming ahead, glanced timidly at the large iron gates that greeted me, and looked skeptically at the large banner above these gates that read: "Welcome to Lewis City Middle School." I walked through, and immediately blinked from the sudden brightness. The sun had come around the horizon, and cut through the thin edge of the school building. The wide sidewalk I was on spanned out in front of me and eventually met what looked like the official entrance to the school building.

Shielding my eyes from the early sun, I hastily hoisted my backpack higher and trotted towards the entrance. As the glass doors swung automatically inwards, I was confronted with a spacious lobby with polished wood floors and, oddly enough, a gorgeously painted ceiling that arched to a dizzying height and from which hung a marvelous chandelier that glinted with the sun's rays as the light entered through impressive skylights. Shielding my eyes again from this dreaded natural light, I clumsily made my way to the front desk which was dead center from me. As I warily made my way into the building, I took in my surroundings and acknowledged the seeming absence of any student life around me. There was no one seated in the lobby, no one making a phone call in the nearby phone booth, no one traversing either of the two large staircases which went off to the right and to the left to the schoolrooms, and no one on campus outside the building...at least from what I'd seen walking in.

But there was someone at the front desk. She was a middle aged lady with a black uniform which had the school's logo branded on the collar. She wore bright red lipstick, and hardly smiled as I arrived at her desk. I noted that her name was J. Simons, noted also that she was staring at me from behind a protective glass wall, and also noted that she wasn't friendly.

"I'm…"

"You're late.".

So that's why there were no students around. "I'm new." I said.

"Mr. Isaacson—?" She began.

"Call me Ishmael." I blurted, but then felt like slapping myself.

The lady J. Simons made no hint of recognition. "Yes," she said, "Obviously." She stood formally. "The school rooms are up the left stairs and past the bathrooms. Your first class will be Math in

Room 132. It started five minutes ago."

I muttered a thank you and skedaddled, feeling angry at myself for appearing so rude at the very start. If I couldn't get myself (including my name) under control I would be toast, and the whole school would despise me. Or maybe I was just being overly pessimistic. I'll admit it, I have those tendencies...most of the time. So when I reached the top of the stairs, and began making my way towards Room 132, I could tell that a feeling of dread was spreading throughout me, and I found myself almost panicking.

Well that definitely wasn't an old feeling.

2. SCHOOL BULLY

I can say this much: At the end of the day, I survived the tormenting stares of the students who obviously despised any new student who walked in their school. Apparently, as much as they cared, anyone who dared be *new* at this school, also dared to step upon their secret base, to trespass upon their sacred school grounds without permission.

But at the end of the day, I escaped in one piece, with my backpack intact, and felt like I couldn't wait till I was in my room with my mom reading Jules Verne out loud, the words of the old writing falling like light warm raindrops upon my listening ears. It was the only thing that felt like my old life, my sweet old life in the country before everything turned unspeakably sour. But even though I tried to leave all my new bad memories at my new school, where I thought all of them were unpleasantly stored, I realized that even the taxi brought a pang of dread, that the speechless taxi driver bespoke untold calamity, and the road home emanated pessimism and deadness. Even when the taxi pulled up to the apartment, the clouds were dull and grey, and the building radiated depression and stood tall and menacing over my head as I entered the underground parking lot. I shifted my backpack uncomfortably over my back, and kept walking, telling myself under my breath that as soon as I reached my room, everything would be fine. Of course, I was only telling myself that.

I pulled myself together as the bare elevator drudged its way up the shafts, humming in a low groan that might have come from a dying man. Its doors opened in a rasp, opening up to a long hallway. I didn't remember the distance being so great, but it seemed like I'd passed a thousand doors before I made it to our own front door, which looked just like all the others, and glared at me from the cracking green faded paint, protesting as I opened it slowly. I found myself looking into our apartment room for the second time in my life, taking in the old and small kitchen with flickering hanging lights, and the small living room which barely fit the TV. I saw my sister sitting there, transfixed to the screen, hardly noticing that I had even walked in. I also registered that my dad had gone to work, probably in one of those skyscrapers I had noticed on my way to school. But where was my mother? I felt a little feeling creeping upon me that perhaps she wasn't here either. But I brushed aside this nagging thought, knowing it was only a symptom of my nerves being on edge, as they had been the whole day. I made my way to my room, which was a very short distance from the front door, and set my backpack against the wall.

It was a small room, letting in a shaft of grey light, revealing a twin-sized bed with superhero themed quilts, pulled neatly over the mattresses, and tucked away underneath my pillow. I smiled, remembering that I had left it messed up that morning, and someone, probably Mother, had fixed them up, as she always had. Back in the days when my bed was in a larger room, back when that room was as old and rustic and known to me as the back of my hand. Those long gone memories of my childhood, which had been snatched away from me as soon as I left them unattended.

But with this knowledge came a fresh wave of grief. It was unexplainable how it came upon me suddenly, and I attributed it to the grey shaft of light coming in from the cracked blinds in my bedroom. So I moved swiftly to the window, taking the blinds and pulling forcefully downwards, blocking out any light from entering, and immersing myself in darkness. Taken aback by the sudden absence of light, I stumbled towards my precious bed lamp, and fumbled with the cord a bit before I had it plugged in, and turned on, shedding a heart-warming glow about the room. I knew it was silly, but the yellow glow of the bulb seemed to momentarily fill my heart up just enough to notice, and then vanish as soon as it had come. I sat hard upon my bed, staring at the opposite wall, wondering how I could escape from the torment of the things I had left behind me. My large country home, my familiar room, my yard of pine trees where I used to play croquet when I had school-breaks. My life had changed, and yet I couldn't put my finger onto what it was exactly that I dreaded most about the change. This part was the most disconcerting to me—for I felt grief like an ocean feels water—and yet could not discern from where it came. But it was upon me, wringing me dry. The shadows in my unfamiliar room lengthened, and I cast my head upon my pillow, only to find a strange, cold pillow that resisted my head as a stone resists the steel of a hammer.

Quite despondent, I wrapped my arms violently around my pillow, as if intending to murder it, but could not even find the strength to do so.

At that instant, I heard footsteps just outside the door. I knew the sound, the rise and fall, the familiar gait. My door opened, the shadows vanished, and there stood my mother, gazing worriedly down at me, and for a brief instant smiled as I looked up. Immediately my room was golden with the glow of my bedside lamp, and the tension that had been building up inside my stomach was relieved.

"How was school?" My mother asked, leaning against the doorframe. That age-old question was one frequented in the days gone by, a familiar item that I had before interpreted as a question, and now associated with a greeting.

"It was fine." That same age-old answer to that same old

question. This time, of course, it was a lie, but how could I not say it? It was built into me, into my very existence.

I reached for my favorite Jules Verne book, perched on the bedside table, and my mother sat beside me in the same place as always. The familiar feel of the pages brushed against my fingers as I found where we had left off in *Journey to the Centre of the Earth*, and handed it to my mother, who took it, and scanned the pages for where she had left off.

"This is where we left off?" She asked.

"Yes," I said, "At least, I think so."

And so it was always — that one traditional exchange — the only echo of my past life.

I lay against my soft pillow, my head sinking slowly into a daydream as my mother started reading, and the sound of her voice filled the room, seeped into my ears. Whether or not she finished the chapter, I don't know. I was fast asleep before she stopped reading. I entered into dreamless slumber.

I woke with a damp chill; My sheet had been pulled over my body, and my bedroom light was off, letting in a cold blue-grey glow through the open windows. Early morning. Tuesday.

I groaned, and pulled the sheets over my head, trying to tell myself that schools didn't exist. As it became very hard to convince myself of this, I shifted restlessly, and finally crawled out of my bed. Standing drowsily for a moment or so, I took in the same book lying atop the side table. Then I came to my senses a little more and decided to find my school backpack. I fumbled with it for a minute, slung it over my shoulder and prepared to walk out the door, when I realized that my pajamas were still on. Sighing inwardly, I turned back to my bedroom to change, thinking how odd it was that my mother hadn't said something about my pajamas before I had *almost* walked out of the door.

I thought this was odd, but then, after changing, I exited my room and learned rather quickly that my mother wasn't in our apartment. Dad had left for work. Only my sister was here. She was busy downing cereal at the kitchen table when I walked up to ask her where Mother was. She didn't look up from her bowl, and it took me a second to realize that she had earbuds in. She hadn't heard me. No matter.

I headed for school. As I always had, I caught a taxi on the side of our apartment's parking lot, and was soon heading for school. That dreaded Lewis City Middle School and that Room 132, and those masses of glaring students. I couldn't figure out which of these made my day. I would soon discover that I had more urgent problems than these alone.

"Ishy!" I heard a taunting voice call out from the end of the corridor. Class had just ended, and I was beginning my ten-minute break just outside of the room when I heard the shout. I pretended at first that I hadn't noticed, reminding myself that my one job on breaks was to be invisible. This didn't work at all. It soon became clear that the shout was directed to me. "Hey Ishy!" I looked up from my lunch, propping myself up against the wall. It was a larger boy, with a rough haircut and a sly grin. He was taller than me by at least a few inches, and his long arms dangled lazily by his side.

"Ishy! Sounds like my sister's name." He jeered at me, as though expecting this to be horrendously insulting. To me it just sounded like he needed to work on better insults.

I simply shrugged. "Wow, you have a sister?" Let's just say it sounded a lot better in my head.

The tall kid stopped in his tracks and slowly drew his eyebrows into a scowl, as though trying to figure out what I'd said.

"I'm Ishmael, by the way." I said bluntly. I went back to my lunch, but could hardly eat anymore. I was watching the kid out of my peripheral vision. I didn't like what I saw.

The tall kid motioned to his right and called to another student. "Hey Duffy."

Duffy, a student who had been leaning all this time against the wall to my right, extracted himself from his pose and joined the tall kid. "Berg." He said. So this apparently was the tall kid's name.

"Get Dan." Berg told Duffy. Duffy was not quite as tall as Berg, and much thinner. He slinked off to get Dan. Duffy returned shortly with the figure of desire—Dan was the shortest, but also the widest. Berg, Duffy, and Dan held a short conference.

The whole ordeal up till now had taken place in under three minutes. I hadn't taken a bite. In my head I was already formulating an escape route. Unfortunately, at Lewis City Middle School, they didn't post escape routes, and I was already regretting it.

The triangle conference of Berg, Duffy, and Dan continued for only a duration of one minute, during which they threw dark glances in my direction and proceeded in their whispers of malcontent and derogatory information. I shrunk against the wall and pretended like I didn't exist. This was a tactic I had tried using the past day or so, and it hadn't worked at all as far as I could tell. This time was no different. Just as I had gathered up the courage to leave, the Triangle of Doom broke, and the three boys eyed me for one dreadful second. Then Berg stepped forward menacingly.

"See here," Berg said. He waved his finger at me and stepped closer. "We deserve respect, don't we?"

I didn't need to answer, for Duffy and Dan were more than happy to oblige him with their fervent head nods. "Respect" they echoed annoyingly.

"You're a newcomer," Berg continued. "You *new* people think you're all that and a bag of chips. You think you're smarter than us. You think you belong here." Berg stepped even closer, and now his lips parted in a malicious sneer and his fist balled and drew itself towards my direction. I could smell his rancid breath, and briefly wondered what he'd eaten earlier for breakfast.

"Well, let me tell you something, *Ishy*." Berg spat. "Newcomers don't belong. *You* don't belong. You're not going to get it easy unless you remember that; give us what we want and give us the respect we deserve." My tensed muscles relaxed minutely as his fist slowly traveled down to his side. But I sensed that Berg wasn't over. Bullies never are, are they?

Berg eyed my backpack, which I had left next to me, leaning against the wall.

"That your backpack?" He snapped. I nodded. "New?" He barked. I shook my head. Berg grunted and grabbed it.

I reacted before I could stop myself. Before I knew it, my right hand was in his face and my left hand was in the process of pulling the backpack from his vice-like grip. I instantly regretted this move. As soon as this had happened, I found myself with my back to the concrete, the evil glare of Berg upon me, and the trickle of something warm running down my face from my nose. I murmured almost incoherently, "...teachers...not getting away with this."

Berg shook his head almost pityingly. "Who would care?"

These parting words were the last thing I heard as my vision dimmed and I blacked out.

After what seemed like a few moments or so, the world began to gradually appear before me. Once everything had cleared, I found that the light being shed on my eyes was not the coarse light from the school building. I breathed in slowly and felt the soft blankets and the feather pillow. I was lying in bed.

3. THE PRINCIPAL

"Please, Mother?" I struggled to sit in my bed, but there was no sufficient headrest and the effort increased the ringing pain in my head. My mother was leaning worriedly against the wall in front of me. In her hand was *Journey to the Centre of the Earth*. When she saw my effort she pushed me softly back into a resting position.

"It gets better in the next chapter," I pleaded again as I saw there might be a chance. There was no other comfort to me than to have a book read aloud; I possessed no video games, and needless to say, we only had one television which was in the living room. I preferred my bed.

For the past two days, I had been marooned in my bedroom since my accident at school, due to tremendous headaches and muscle stiffness. I could not fathom how such a small accident would be the cause of my continued absence from school, but the reality was that Berg, Duffy and Dan were gone from my life, if but for a few days, and the monotony of classes, stoic teachers, and malignant stares of alienating students were gone, if but for the time being. I was safe, at least, for as long as my pain persisted. That alone was enough to be satisfied with. Yet my only respite was when I drifted off to dreamless sleep, and my body ached with nerveless ecstacy, though this desirable condition of slumber lasted but for what seemed a fraction of a second, and I would awaken again a few hours later. The easiest way to fall asleep was to continue through the work that the author of a book had written about a fascinating fiction in a different land of which I could imagine I was a part. You could say that a book read aloud was my method of escape. Thus, it was also my newfound foundation of existence; before, a relaxing commodity, now, a life-saver, just as any drug would be to the human body and mind.

My pleading finally paid off. My mother sighed and sat on the edge of my bed, opening the book for the fifth time that day. Now it was evening, and bound to be the last reading of the day. But this chapter was the perfect closer — the section of the book where the trio of explorers' wanderings finally pay off and they discover that there had been all this time an ancient land of paradise existing beneath mankind, at the center of the world. My eyes were initially widened as my mother read, gazing upwards and painting in my mind's eye the language of the novel onto the canvas of the ceiling: The lush hillsides, the rolling sand, the glistening water. It was as if the characters had escaped from the regulations, schools and society, leaving their memories of darkness behind them, and treading obliviously into the light. As my mother continued to read, and the characters in the story entered their dream world, I also entered into mine; yet my dream world was full of dark and shadows, much like the mysterious cave tunnels that had followed the characters Otto, Axel, and Hans into the gaping abyss of the earth.

"Isaacson?"

The world formed before my eyes.

"Isaacson!" A blunt and rapid sort of exclamation, obviously from an adult.

I opened my eyes wider and tried to understand where I was. That part didn't take long; I was in class, and had obviously drifted off to sleep in the middle of a lecture.

"Hm?" I muttered, and shifted in my seat.

"The War of the Roses started *when* and lasted *how long?*"

Yep, caught sleeping in history class. I had probably been asked this question for that very reason. But that was usual. It seemed that not only students, but also teachers, had reason to despise me and thus pick on me whenever the opportunity presented itself.

Well, what was there to do but answer?

"Started in Europe." I replied just as bluntly. "Ended after the fighting had stopped."

It's not like I had expected it to go well, right? Well it was worse than that. Worse than I had expected it to be. Something that had to do with the principal's office, and, "because of the lack of a school therapist," a long speech from someone who had obviously never practiced talking in front of a mirror, but deigned fit the right to do so because of their position of authority over me, which had ended in a questionnaire that pertained to the aforementioned speech, which I unfortunately flunked. Yes, my "misconduct" in class did not go as I had expected. After I flunked the Principal's Office, my mother was called. I could hear her voice on the end of the line as though from a great distance away, and I could hear much clearer the tight and maintained voice of the principle as he informed my mother that I was being sent home early, and that I deserved some sort of lesson before being sent back, and that if I did return, I was expected to perform at a higher standard than I had apparently been exhibiting of late.

At every blow I shrunk into my chair. At every angry syllable and gesture, I felt smaller.

I heard my mother at this time bring up the bullies at school. Again.

"With the way Ishmael has been acting, I would be surprised if such activity didn't happen more often," the principal retorted. With every depreciating glance from the stern face of the principle, I felt more and more like what I had felt when I had been lying on the cold cement of the school corridor, with Berg standing over me, and that cold judgement that still echoed in my brain. "Who would care?"

"If he can't meet our objectives here at school, then frankly we don't want him anymore." This was the eventual sum-up of the phone conversation with my mom, and I was sent home.

My mother said little of the conversation that day, and said nothing to me in light of what had just happened. She only read another chapter from our book, after which I fell asleep.

In the morning, I went straight back to school, only to find the situation worse.

The first classroom door was closed when I arrived, even though I was five minutes early. It was opened by the teacher, who when he saw me, offered a look of distaste but opened the door wider to let me through. After this, I was almost escorted by the teacher to an empty seat in the front row, in which I seated myself and then quickly realized that Teacher had knowingly begun the math lecture without me, five minutes early, and just as quickly found out that I was to be the person called upon to answer any question that the teacher so desired to ask of me. These answers were generally wildly invented, and apparently pertained to that section of lecture that I had conveniently missed upon my so-called 'late' arrival. ("What number of elves were present at the aforementioned party if there were twelve orcs handing out the juice punch?") Upon the third time of me being called upon, and not knowing the answer (the question being "If 6 of the orcs left the juice punch table, and immediately killed 7 ravens, what number of mushrooms were eaten in total?"), I responded matter of factly that perhaps another student smarter than I could find it within themselves to answer the question whose answer seemed obvious to everyone else. The math teacher, livid with rage, commissioned me to the principal's office with the complaint that I was a poor student entirely devoid of any respect for superiors, and must be punished by reciting the preamble to the Constitution five times in front of the whole class when I had returned from the judgement of the principle who shared similar feelings about me. The rest of the day went just as well.

I find it impossible for anyone to blame me for feeling an utter sense of misplacement. A deep feeling of not belonging anywhere.

I, Ishmael: the outsider. Lost, as though belonging to no one.

But then, at the end of the day, as always, there was a fortress, my bedroom, and of course, my mother, with a book in her hand and a boundless sympathy, such that I hoped it was impossible for me to feel hopeless anymore, as I leaned against the pillow, and stared at the wall in front of me, waiting to hear what my mother would say.

There she was, holding the book; but it was dropped to her side, and she was leaning as she typically did against my door frame, gazing down at me. That weary grey bleakness about my room hung around me.

"So the principal again?" She asked.

"Yeah."

There was a pause.

"You were being disrespectful during class?" She asked. There was no accusation in her tone.

I shook my head bleakly.

There was a pause. She tilted her head to the ground, as though deep in thought. Her brows drew together in a slight frown.

"Mom?" I asked, as though to reassure myself that she still knew I was here. But the shadows in my room lengthened and she seemed to pull away from me, and I felt as though we were divided by a transparent curtain of impenetrable glass. "It isn't true." I stabbed the cruel silence. "They all hate me — I didn't do anything!" This sounded ridiculous and unconvincing coming out of my mouth, but it seemed to matter little — she voiced no objection, nor did she reply. Now she moved to put her arm about me, and I collapsed into her embrace.

18

4. More Bruises

The Berg, Duffy, and Dan trio did nothing to lighten my burden; nor did it seem that they could, of their own volition, as it remained that they were an inseparable portion of my troubles. It would be hardly encompassing enough to merely explain them away as the *beginning,* or *herald* of my demise, since now they only represented to me my present darkness, a mere image of something within, a fresh layer of black paint on a mangled canvas of sorrows. This understanding was deeply inexplicable, and I never hoped to know why such ponderings invaded my subconscious. However, it goes without saying that they did their best to make me quite miserable, and I loathed them to no end, and spent my few free hours at school entertaining whimsical fantasies of holding Berg down on asphalt and wringing the lifeblood from his body. The reality was, of course, relatively disheartening, seeing that even if some demonic will spontaneously took a hold of me, I could not, to save my own skin, grab a hold of Berg and even slightly throw him off balance. I shouldn't have to explain that Berg was of a sturdier build, taller, and seemed unreasonably accustomed to surprise attacks from enemies, of which I am quite sure he had many. And then, even if I were strong enough to confront Berg during one of his daily torments, I could not question the impaling presence of his sudden allies, Duffy, and Dan. In fact, their alliance suggested to me that nearly every student at my school would side with Berg if he so much as snapped his fingers. In this light, my situation was most undesirable of all undesirables. You understand why I referenced school as a prison, of which I was a despondent inhabitant.

Even now, as routine would have it, I spied Berg eyeing me, from my awkward position against one of the many stucco walls that comprised the school building. I quickly consumed what was left of my sandwich as I saw him approach.

"Ishy!" Berg spat.

"*Ishmael.*"

"Ishy-mayel." Berg's pace didn't check. Now he was a foot away from my face, and I could feel his breath. I was used to feeling his breath several times a day. I glanced both ways down the hall, and felt little surprise that they had been suddenly emptied of students and all other life forms. It was just me and Berg. Duffy and Dan weren't currently in the picture. Maybe they were terrorizing another unfortunate student. Odd, because it was very hard for me to picture anyone half as unfortunate as I, at the moment.

"Got the money?" Berg spat. I felt the spit.

"What money?" Best to stall.

"Oh I don't know," Berg mocked in a high-pitched voice, "maybe the money *you promised to bring?*" His fingers locked around my collar. Maybe stall more.

My face must have looked quite pale, and I could feel my stomach churning. My arms shook as I grasped for dear life onto Berg's arm. I tried desperately to stop them from shaking.

"Oh, the money that I promised to bring as long as you'd stop beating me up? Well I haven't got it."

It took some time for Berg to contemplate this. "Why not?" His eyebrows drew together as he pondered the meaning of this information, possibly not able to figure out any reasonable scenario in which someone didn't do exactly what he wanted.

I leaned away from him, against the wall. Berg pulled me back. His grey eyes were little slivers that seemed cut out of his cold scarred face. A face with too many scars for a teenager. I briefly wondered how he happened by them, if he hadn't done it himself.

"Listen," I struggled back against Berg's vice grip on my collar. Nothing doing. "There's no way to get you money, 'cause I don't have any!"

Berg stared at me unbelieving. "No money?" was all he could say.

I swallowed. My parents never gave me money. Maybe they didn't trust me. Or maybe I hadn't earned it? Or both. I shook my head. Berg's eyes narrowed even more until I could barely see the gray little glints, beaming straight into my wide blue ones. Then, instantly, the dreaded moment came. Berg grabbed a hold of my shirt with both hands, and swung me away from the stucco wall with brute force, preparing to nail me once again into the floor, another broken nose, another week's rest in bed, another week away from school. But for a brief moment, my mind flew towards salvation.

"Wait!" I cried, and Berg wrenched me back upright. My feet tripped and caught at the ground, trying to maintain balance. He towered over me, dangling me from his hands, as he eyed me. "I'll do anything else!" I vomited up the words before I could think twice. I bit my lip after saying this. But it had the desired effect. Berg set me back on my feet, keeping his hand clamped onto my collar. I briefly wondered if we had a clothing iron back at the apartment. Somehow, at that moment, that seemed of the utmost importance. It took me a few seconds to get my priorities straight.

"You'll do — anything else?" Berg interrogated, confused.

"Anything." I said. *Anything other than breaking my nose again.*

Berg stared at me for a good minute. I stared back for a little less than a minute — which gave me enough time to regret my decision.

But then he spoke. And it was the oddest thing, because it sounded like he was reading off a script. His voice became duller and more monotonous, and he began, "down this road," here, he gestured down the stretch of road adjacent to the school, in the opposite direction of my family's apartment, "for about a mile, you'll see a house — you can't miss it — well, it's haunted," here I smirked at him, "take my word for it," Berg persisted, "it is." He stared at me some more to get this point across.

"Ok, ok," I said, "So it's haunted — which of course, just proves you're an idiot — so what have I got to do with it?"

"You," said Berg pointedly, "are going to go into that house *alone*, find a certain object, and come back here, and show me. Otherwise I wouldn't know whether you'd actually been there or not."

I waited for more, but Berg had apparently finished. I laughed out loud, suddenly feeling that weight from my chest lift, even though Berg was still holding on to my collar. That was it? That was all he had for me to do? But then I remembered those things called Darkness and Being Alone, and something occurred to me about ambushes, and a dizzying feeling came upon me, such that I cannot quite explain it. A bit of a cold sensation, that started in my head and moved swiftly downwards until it drenched my entire body. I went quite limp with fear. Me go into an abandoned house *alone*? And what kind of trap did Berg have up his sleeve this time? Fear-driven resolve took a grasp at my neck.

I practically spat in his face. "'Fraidy-cat. Go boil your head."

Berg shook with rage. Then he took my shoulders with both hands and slammed my unsurprised countenance onto the concrete flooring. My mind went dark.

I awoke to my room of dimly lit walls and popcorn ceiling. I had been placed flat on my back, and as soon as I regained complete wakefulness, pain from the bruising coursed throughout my nervous system. I tediously shifted myself onto my side and the pain in my shoulder blades jumped and spasmed, but eventually diminished enough for me to think clearly. The back of my head had also dug into the concrete when Berg nailed me, and the reminder was shooting through my skull. I lifted my head a few inches off the pillow, and turning, noticed that there was a scarlet stain on the pillowcase.

My mother came in, as she usually did when I was so incapacitated, but this time, I noticed that she was silent, and did not ask me questions about what had happened to me. Mouth sealed, she busied herself by flitting in and out, much like a shadow, appearing for a second to open my window, letting in some head-splitting light that did not bode well with the pain, and then vanishing again. Once she was gone, I was left in utter silence, even though my bedroom door was wedged slightly open. I wondered briefly what silent activity my family was engaged in outside my room. I assumed that my sister was playing a game with headphones in, and my mom was shopping. But then she entered my room again to refill the water in my water cup, which stood on my bedside table. I couldn't let her leave this time.

"Mom," I managed, my throat crying out in protest. It was dry as a bone.

There it was — the change, she looked up from her task, and her features softened.

"Book."

"I'm glad you're feeling better already," she said somewhat cheerfully, but not making any move towards Jules Verne.

I decided not to argue directly with her concerning my physical wellbeing. I certainly wasn't feeling better; in fact, sleep had suited me much better than consciousness, and the pain in my back had become a dull throbbing sensation, shooting up my spine with each miniscule movement. "The bruises..." I murmured, wincing as the pain shot up my spine again.

"You need some sleep," she said, as she sat on the side of my bed. This time, her composure was more gravitational, and she leaned towards me, concern written across the lines in her forehead. "This..." her hand touched my back, a rather bruised part that protested painfully when she pressed on it, "Remember what we talked about, Ishmael?"

"About what...?" I followed her hand with my eyes now as it made its way back to safety.

"I'm getting calls every day from your principal. Mr. Burns is concerned about your...behaviour."

"*My*...behavior?" I tried to conceal the revulsion in my tone. "Berg...big kid...he shoved me — it was hard flooring, concrete..."

"We can't have more trouble," my mother's expression of concern was even more tangible as I viewed from the corner of my peripheral vision. Her hand went on my shoulder again, a different part, and perhaps she didn't know that there was a large cut there — a large cut and a large bruise underneath. Certainly she couldn't have felt the new spike of pain that saturated my body, pulling all my muscles into one nauseating contraction. "You know I only want what's best for you...more trouble could mean you getting expelled." Then she quickly stood, glanced worriedly my way, and left the room.

Darkness closed on my mind, partly from the pain, and partly from the severe injustice. It was not the first time my mom had bought in to the story the principal gave her, no doubt after being lied to by Berg. A story spun, no doubt involving me attacking a helpless and innocent Berg, whose friends came to his rescue and pummeled me before I released him. That story would explain my bruises. But it was unlike my mother to move with this tide, to listen to the whispers emanating from the dark corners of my world, the shadows I tried to leave behind, hoping she could wipe them away. Instead of eradicating this threat, she had stood by, a mere observer, effectively sending me back, back to the terrorization of Berg, Duffy, and Dan, back to that hell pit of Mr. Burns, the prejudiced teachers, and their sneering students.

As her steps faded down the hall, darkness closed over my senses, and I welcomed the relief that unconsciousness brought. But before it took me completely, my mind was formulating a plan. I knew, of course, deep down, what must happen. What had to happen. I had to do what Berg wanted. I had to make things worse. Then she would see just how dark my world was.

Then, only then, could she rescue me from it.

5. The Haunted House

"Hey Berg!" I taunted from across the field. The sun shone through the crevices of the tall school building, cutting into my eyes. But I could still make out the hulking figure of Berg across the way. As soon as I'd shouted his name, his back stiffened, and his body surged upright, head tilting my direction. And there were the inaudible footsteps as he lumbered towards me, followed closely by Duffy and Dan. It seemed like a couple seconds before they were upon me. Berg grabbed me by the arm as soon as I was in reach. That guy didn't waste any time.

"Oh yeah, Ishy?" He grunted, "Have something you want to tell me?"

I stiffened instinctively as soon as his hand tightened its steel grip on my forearm. I attempted a leer. "Yeh. Sure do."

"How was the haunted house, Ishy? Get scared?"

"Of course I wasn't *scared*." I spat in his face. "Any baby *would*, though."

"Did you find the paper?"

"The what - ?" Of course. The item he'd asked me to retrieve. I hadn't. Because I hadn't gone there.

Berg's features stiffened in an internal fit of rage. But oddly enough, his face relaxed after a second or two had passed. His rage was replaced by a sneer, an ungodly thing that possessed the corners of his mouth and made his eye twitch. The effect was surreal to say the least.

"Describe it to me."

"Describe…?" I wondered out loud. Oh. The haunted house.

"The haunted house of course — describe it to me. What was it like?" Berg was still standing, holding onto my arm in a vice-like grip.

"Of course," I said, putting on the pose of one who is extremely confident in himself. Of course, it was hard to achieve this look since Berg was grappling my arm, and so the pose came out as a very awkward attempt to defy gravity. My mind was reeling, trying to figure out what a haunted house should look like. "You know…" I said good-naturedly, "It was…it definitely looked haunted, that's for sure. You were right."

Berg's gaze pierced through my skull, and I felt an inexplicable responsibility to wither and die, but I held on to the life that I had.

"*What did it look like?*" Berg growled.

"Oh, you know…" I began, searching for answers.

"*Tell me.*" Berg pulled me threateningly close to his massive form. For the first time I noticed what a dark and cavernous void his mouth was, and what dreadful pits his eyes were — cavernous and dark just like his mouth.

"Dark!" I said before Berg could decide whether or not to break my nose. "And cavernous!"

Berg's head tilted to one side. "Cavernous?"

"Yes!" I leapt at the opportunity. "You know, it was a regular haunted house, as you probably know, it was dark brown, chipped wood, the windows were all fogged up, and the front yard was more like a graveyard. I'm pretty sure…" As I'd hoped, Berg's grin drew wider and wider as I said all this, revealing more of the awful space behind it, revealing the gargantuan and oddly proportioned teeth. "The grass was pretty darn brown, but the inside was even worse, 'cause there weren't any doors, and there was just a bunch of creaking and groaning...probably the wind. But you know how it is with haunted stuff." I finished my little informative speech, and prepared myself for what would come next.

"Well I'll be damned," Berg's mouth had now officially widened the widest I could reasonably fathom it widening. His breath was twice as bad as it had been yesterday, and I not only wondered what he'd eaten for breakfast, but also briefly pondered if he had parents. "Give yerself a pat on the back, Ishy." I decided against it, given my precarious position — hovering above the cement, all my weight being held in midair by Berg's superhuman left hand. "Time to give you what you deserve, by rights."

I watched, helplessly hanging in the air, as a flash of metal appeared in Berg's right hand, glinting its razor-sharp blade in the cutting sunlight. And the knife seemed more a part of Berg than it did of itself, a representation of all Berg's evil. But Berg himself seemed more a part of hell than he was of himself, more of a representation of my paranoia and fear, more a characteristic of my darkness and dread, than a separate entity. Duffy and Dan roughly clutched my shoulders, and Berg came at me with his knife. But it was not Berg and his knife coming at me as much as it was darkness and fear approaching, not as much Berg seizing my arm as it was my worst nightmare threatening to drown me, to kill me where I stood. Berg hissed in my ear, and it was as though the only thing I had of value in life had been ruthlessly snatched from me. "You see," he began, and I immediately broke into a cold sweat. "The haunted house doesn't *have* chipped wood." I felt his dank and humid breath perpetrating my senses, "There is no graveyard. The windows are spotless. The house is in excellent condition, with light green wood panelling. The inside of the house is large but comfortable, with expensive furniture, and a tiled kitchen. It has a nice large chandelier in the living room, and bedrooms that have light blue walls.

Oh, and it has a fireplace." The sunlight was getting too bright, and I squeezed my eyes shut, trying to block the light, trying to hide, but it was cutting through me, cutting me open, trying to get inside — "It doesn't seem haunted," Berg went on, "That's because it isn't haunted at all." Why was Berg telling me this? Why was his voice unlike how I'd ever heard it before, grating and low, as though a different person was talking? And why did he have that knife in his hand still? Now he brought the steel to my bare arm. "Just a few cuts on each arm should do it," he said, and I instantly felt the pain, felt the metal rending my skin apart, felt the blood pouring down my arm, dripping off my fingertips. Berg repeated the cut a few inches above the original, and I felt the blood draining away, felt my world slipping away — and somehow, quite unexplainably, felt the pain washing away. It was as though my insides were being emptied, and now I felt lightheaded and relaxed. Cut after cut, and now repeated on my left arm, cut after cut jogged my feelings, lifting me higher and higher. The sensation of leaving my blood on the ground, my body leaving the ground behind, the wind on my face…

But then the next words out of Berg's mouth brought back the pain, the feeling of blood drenching my arms, the wind on my face from Berg's nauseating breath, "That should be enough to get to your momma, shouldn't it...*Ishmael?*"

Now I was falling. My body fell towards the ground as Berg released his grasp. My mind fell towards the ground, and passed it, continuing to fall, leaving the ground behind, plummeting further and further into a bottomless chasm. The falling sensation did not fade, and I did not wake to my warm bed, did not wake to the dimly lit bedroom, did not wake to a pain in my back, in my head, in my arm, in my soul; I kept falling. Now there were flashes of light in this bottomless chasm. These flashes of light were thoughts, and they flew by me as I fell at an

immeasurable speed. *That was the first time Berg called me by my full name.*
The flickers of light were biting, grinding, one moment, gone the next,
fading into the distance. *How did Berg know about my mom?* And now a
flash of light appeared but did not fade like the rest. It maintained its
glimmer, falling with me as I fell at a dizzying pace. Now the wave of
light encapsulated me and I was sucked into its thought:

*I was in a large bed, a bed I did not recognize, staring at the wall in front
of me, a pale blue wall, a different shade from the dull brown back at our
apartment. Then movement from the corner of my eye. I turned my head. Mother.
But something was different. Much different. She was...she looked...older. Her face
was a pale white, with a few premature wrinkles lining the surface of her forehead.
Her head was wrapped with a white handkerchief, and she leaned against my wall
as though it were the only thing keeping her from fainting from the exertion of
keeping herself upright. Something was off...but I couldn't put my finger on it. And
then she spoke. Her voice was faint and soft.*

"How was school?"

"It was fine." I felt myself saying, not of my own will, as though in a
dream.

*Now she moved to the side of my bed and sat on the edge, precariously,
unsteadily. Her chest rose and fell with effort, but she reached across and pulled a
book from the bedside table as though it took little strain. She flipped to the page
with the red bookmark. It was a rough, folded paper bookmark, more of a
makeshift placeholder than anything else.*

*"This is where we left off?" There it was, a question I had heard recently,
but in a different room, a different place.*

*"Yes," I heard myself replying, "At least, I think so." That same answer.
One I had replied not a few days ago, after I had been injured by Berg at school.
And then I heard my mother begin to read, heard the words pour out with her
fading voice, caught the story as it was being told. It was* Journey to the Center
of the Earth. *And it was that very chapter she had read me not three days ago —
the chapter when Otto, Axel and Hans reach paradise, and find the vast expanse of*

ocean in the middle of the earth.

"It was quite an ocean," she read, "with the irregular shores of earth, but desert and frightfully wild in appearance…"

But then her words faded from me, and everything became dark. I became once more conscious of the fact that I was still falling down a bottomless chasm.

6. THE KNIFE

My reality painfully rushed back. I wasn't falling, but I hadn't landed either, and I felt suspended in an indefinite limbo until my room faded into view. When the dim morning light from the window became evident to me, the pillow suddenly felt like a pillow, and my sheets felt like cloth. I was back in my bedroom, the dark brown one, not the one with blue walls from my imagination. I stared up at my popcorn ceiling, searching for answers, waiting for a sign, longing for an explanation. My fall down the chasm must have taken me through the entire night, and now it was morning again. I lay for quite some time, and during that expansive amount of waiting, no answers were found, no signs appeared, and no explanation presented itself. Though I felt the bed solidly beneath me, and perceived the glow from both my bedside lamp and my window, I might as well have been still falling down that bottomless chasm, for confusion and anxiety set in. I thought back to my expenditure with Berg at school. I had desired for my mother to truly see my plight, the extent to which the malice had gone, but had not expected Berg to close in so suddenly, carry that ghastly switchblade, and cut so deep. His words still rang through my senses, *"That should be enough to get to your momma, shouldn't it...Ishmael?"* Not only was it thoroughly discombobulating that Berg had called me by my full name, but what was more disheartening was Berg's grasp of my situation. Berg had not only penetrated into my life at school, he had (perhaps unwittingly) exposed an area of my life I had no idea he was aware of. True, perhaps I was getting too far ahead of myself, and Berg was only assuming what any bully would — that any kid like me would go crying to their mommy and tell a sob-story about how they were bullied at school. But Berg couldn't have possibly known that I was intending to use him to appeal to my mother's good nature. And he'd said enough for me to suspect as much. But then the absurdity of the notion struck me at that moment, and I realized that Berg had no way of knowing what went on in my head, and anything he'd said had been of pure coincidence; any sly remark, threat or attack was meant to appeal to my already far-spun paranoia. So I hoped. But I could never really know for sure, and one of the things about paranoia is that it never drops what it picks up. So I clung to the thought I was thinking, regardless of the terrifying prospect of its truthfulness.

I began thinking about Berg's monologue, an arduous and thoroughly petrifying one, all the more so because I had no idea why he'd even said what he said in the first place. While restraining me, Berg had inasmuch described the "haunted house" he'd mentioned before, and then went on to inform me that it wasn't haunted, after all. All this amounted to my desperate confusion, and my incomprehensive conclusion that he was ever more a control-freak than I suspected, and enjoyed knowing things I didn't, lying to me, and then informing me of his deception. Berg was like all bullies, after all, a simple-minded fool who acquired pleasure by confusing his victims. He was quite successful in that respect. But not, perhaps, as successful as he was at inflicting pain and injury on my body. Now my thoughts flew to the present, and I moved my arms weakly. That was when I figured out that they were completely covered in bandages. White linen wrappings encapsulated my arms from my elbows to my wrist, and as I moved my arms to test their remaining strength, I felt the sting of the wounds, the deep incisions that had been made on both arms. I wasn't even quite certain as to the exact number of cuts Berg had decided to make on each arm, but felt sure that there were at least a few on each. Apparently my mother had bandaged my arms while I had been passed out, or whatever it was that had happened to my brain.

As little tingling pains ran up my arms, I slowly smiled. My plan had worked thus far. Berg had done exactly what I'd wanted him to, maybe even a little better than I had expected — the knife was an unforeseen but lucky happening. Now I was cut and bleeding. My mother would withhold me from school to spare me from further injury. It's what my mother would do, because she cared about my well-being more than she did my school status. Berg, Duffy, Dan, the hellish teachers and the students they taught, would be gone from my life. Forever.

As I looked about me and came even more slowly to my senses, another thing relieved my anxiety. That Thought, of course, had been just that: a thought; my bedroom walls were not blue. I looked around and noticed that my bed wasn't as large as I had seen in the Thought, and when Mother came in, her head wasn't wrapped in a stupid handkerchief. Not that I expected it to be real. It was just relieving knowing it wasn't. For sure. But if I had expected comfort from her entrance, the feeling did not come. Had I expected it? Her face was stiff, her expression like that on a canvas — once formed, immobile, impassive. Not that she didn't have an expression — the expression of concern — but it was a painted concern, an emotion that had been molded by the creator's hands and did not retain the moldability of the hands that had formed them. Instead, the molded clay became rock solid, stale...lifeless?

She sat near me, on the edge of the bed, which gave slightly, and I felt the mattress pull beneath me. Yet she was distant. I imagined the sculptor placing his molded sculpture behind a wall of glass, for onlookers to gaze at but never to touch, to glorify but never to hold.

Her arm reached towards me, and it seemed at that moment as though she were reaching to me from another world, a distant place much different from the cold dismal place I inhabited. Her arm rested lightly on my shoulder, her expression of concern still fixed upon her face. She shook her head. "Ishmael, Ishmael." Her voice was soft, and I felt it like a whisper in the dark. "Ishmael." And then she just looked at me for a long time, somewhat wistfully, as though contemplating something far far beyond. I hoped she was thinking of my cuts, thinking of that hated Berg, thinking of my school, thinking of calling the principal, holding me back, keeping me safe at home. Thinking about something. But instead she continued shaking her head, her expression of concern etched all the more deeper into her forehead. "I always knew school was rough, Ishmael," she said. My eyes darted towards hers, waiting for her to say it. Waiting to say those magic words. "But I never knew you were…" she stopped talking suddenly, as though the words were caught in her throat, as though she were about to say something profoundly horrible and couldn't bear the thought of saying it out loud. "…harming yourself." And there, she had said it, the words had surfaced, and they came at me like knives, sinking into my heart. "I didn't know, Ishmael," she said, and now were those tears threatening to surface? She clutched my hand. "You should have said something…about what you were going through."

Now the pain in my chest contorted and tears began welling up in my eyes. My vision clouded, and my mother became a blur. I shook my head feebly. "No, mom, you don't understand, don't understand anything…"

"I know how hard it is to tell me," my mother said, as though she truly understood what I was trying to say. Her next words were spoken slowly, as though she were thinking carefully about each one.

"We're going to see a man today. You and me, Ishmael. After school. You can tell him."

My head fell back into my pillow. I clenched my eyes shut, trying to block all the light, trying to block all the words, trying to block my mother from my sight. Anger replaced them, spilling in like liquid fire, rising up, eating everything it touched and turning all to ash.

"Ishmael?"

No. This answer surfaced with fiery vigor in my brain. What did it mean? *No.* I squeezed my eyes harder but now there were flashes of light, briefly illuminating my darkness, vanishing just as quickly as they'd come. My mother had said my name again, and it echoed as though from the other end of the chasm. *No.* I had bottled this deep down, further and further, until I had lost it, did not know what it was, until now. It had been graven in me since as long as I can remember, a hatred, an anger, an unspeakable fury, graven onto my heart like the words Lewis City Middle School were graven into the ancient stone. *No.* A retort, a horrendous retort as though it came from Berg's sneering features. *No.* A distaste, a disdain that made me think of the school principal, glaring at me from across the desk, hating me, loathing me, wanting me dead — except this feeling was coming from inside *me.* And finally...*No.* A cold, removed feeling surfaced within me, the cold uncaring feeling of Berg, as he'd nailed me to the ground, that cold, unfeeling… *"Who would care?"* And there it was, Berg's voice echoing in my head, surging up from within me, surging up with the liquid fire, shredding away the flashes of light.

I opened my eyes half-way, letting the tears mix into my whirlpool of emotions, letting the world in front of me blur so I didn't have to look her in the eye, but letting my voice ring clear. "NO!" I screamed. My mother's blurred figure stood up quickly. My vocal chords shredded under the duress, "This isn't *me,* it's not my fault, but you *don't care, do you?* If you did...none of this would have happened!"

And Mother looked at me behind her transparent wall with a gaze that snuck like night into my little heart, that ground my bones like broken glass, that seemed to re-open the lacerations on my arms. She looked at me for this awful moment, a moment in which the world seemed to stand still, where there was just a frozen moment of anger and pain, and then she was gone.

I threw my sheets from my sweat-soaked body, trying to throw the darkness away, throw the fear away. The fear of my anger. I wanted it to own me. I flew to my drawer, opening it, as though expecting myself to open a solution, to find the Answer. Or maybe just to find my precious book before my mother could take it, take it far away, take it and lock it in a dark, dark cabinet of splintered wood and solid steel. My drawer flew open, and a glint of metal met my eyes as it flew open, stopping with a jolt as the wood hit my chest, making a hollow, empty sound. And the clink of metal. Of the something inside. And as I looked inside the cabinet, I saw it. I saw what my mother had somehow been trying to tell me, saw the glint and the wetness, the glint and the wetness together, the silver and red, the red coating the silver, almost covering it, leaving a red shine, a blood-red shine…

It was Berg's switchblade. In my cabinet.

I felt a flurry, a maelstrom of feelings, such that I could not discern where one ended and the other began, could not choose the feeling I wanted to feel. But I knew the impossible had happened, that thing I had wished for, deep, deep down in my mind, ever since my anger for Berg had reached its apparent exhaustion. Of course, I had thought it had been exhausted, but now it was as if some demonic will *had*, after all, taken a hold of me. This volition reached its long gnarled arm out of my maelstrom of emotions and took hold of me. And I took a hold of the knife. It would end. Had to end. For my sake. No, for my mother's sake. Not only had Berg continued his harm to me, he had proceeded further and attempted to frame me for my own harm. I would unveil this deception Berg had placed upon my mother, wipe Berg away from my blackened canvas of sorrows, extinguish the consuming flame that had come into my life with Berg and his hated school. It was about time to go to school. And so I did. With the switchblade, still covered with blood, concealed in my front pocket.

It felt like not a moment had passed, and already I was striding up the path to the school courtyard, to the place where the students were dropped off before class, gathering into their little social circles of which I was never a part, gathering together and looking at me, looking at Berg, silently taunting, whispering, shooting malicious glares with their empty, soulless eyes. I strode up to the courtyard, into the middle of the groups, the middle of the students, the middle of the field. I almost became conscious of their glares, their faces, their little imbecilic voices. But before they could reach me, I blocked them. I blocked them from my senses, blackened them out, silenced them. I was headed in a straight line, because of course I knew where he was. I knew where he always waited. And today was no different; Berg was there. And he was waiting. He was standing with his arms crossed, facing my direction, knowing exactly when I would arrive, expecting it, grinning evilly like always. Of course, he couldn't know. For the first time at this school, I felt a warm feeling spreading up my chest, traveling up my neck, bringing a hint of a grin to my face. I felt smug. Confident. Berg wouldn't know that I was carrying his switchblade. Certainly wouldn't know why I was still walking straight towards him, closing the gap at an incredible speed. Certainly he wouldn't know why my right hand now went to my front pocket as I strode towards him. Wouldn't know until it was too late. And it certainly *didn't* appear as though he was aware of my intention. Until I was within ten feet of him — then he did something that I'd never seen Berg do. He let his hands fall to his side, and his expression became insanely relaxed. Well...good. He wasn't ready, he was too self-confident, thought he could take me with his fists. I was five feet away from him. I grasped the handle of the switchblade, pulled it out of my pocket, felt the cool steel of the handle against my clutching hand. And I watched Berg's expression, which oddly enough didn't sway or falter when he noticed that I was holding his switchblade. And it made me hate him even more.

"YOU'RE DONE!" I screamed. "YOU STAY AWAY!" And then I jumped on him. I felt the handle in my hand, felt the *swish* of the blade as it unsheathed.

Felt like I was cutting butter as I slammed it into Berg's chest. And Berg's expression didn't falter. He didn't look surprised, still grinning at me, grinning that hellish grin, that smug, hellish grin. I stood there with the knife in his chest, feeling his blood draining down the handle of the knife, coating my hands. Not a moment ago, I had justified this violence with my immense hatred towards Berg. Of course, now I was confused. I was confused, because as I looked into Berg's empty eyes, into his grinning face, I realized that I didn't hate him. Not really. My demonic will, my fiery passion, my earnest grip on the knife handle was fueled by another anger. An anger towards my mother. This revelation altered nothing, and I pressed the switchblade harder, pressed my face closer to his ear so that he could hear me past the noise of Death.

"We're done playing this game."

And Berg still looked at me, that smug look on his face. Now his hands raised to mine, and he clutched my arms with his vice-like grip, beginning to shake his head "Oh no, Ishy," His grinning face said, *"You're* not finished." And then with his brute force I had grown to know too well, he gripped both my hands which were wrapped around the handle of the knife. Then with a sudden vigor, he pulled. He pulled the knife deeper, deeper in, further, and further, until my hands were inside, and then I was inside, and I was falling.

Into the chasm.

7. THE NIGHTMARE

You probably know what it's like to have a dream, a dream where you fall out your apartment window, jump out of your tree house, or ride your bike off a cliff. If so, you probably know the feeling of falling, when the ground rushes at you. Except you never meet the ground. Your surroundings grow dark, and you wake up safe in your bed, relieved that it was all just a dream. So maybe you don't know what it's like to never wake up, but instead, to keep falling, feeling that emptiness in your chest, but feeling it stay there forever, pulling and eating at you.

As I fell, I received no such consolation of most dreamers, because I did not know where I was, did not know how long I would fall, did not know if I was dreaming, in order to be able to wake up in the first place. I wasn't merely falling; I was being dragged down, pulled downwards as Berg had pulled his knife through his chest, an act I could never reconcile to myself, could never hope to grasp. Maybe a part of me wanted to kill Berg myself. However, another part of me didn't want to kill Berg at all, and I had simply assigned Berg the name of all my troubles, the part of me that had rushed to kill him. But I did wonder, as I continued to fall into black infinitum, if Berg was, in fact, the name of all my troubles, or if I had simply fabricated this concept.

My troubles hadn't begun with Berg, after all. They had begun the moment we left Home, the moment we'd moved. Moved from our country home, my familiar school, my familiar world.

Now the flashes of light came again. Light contortions of Thought, convulsing in the darkness, expanding and contracting, flashing in and out, entering and exiting with rapid brilliance, washing my brain in a wave and then submerging it in blackness just as quickly. These waves of consciousness were periodic, spasmodic, and thus meaningless, too short-lived to be understood, doing nothing but discombobulating me even further, to an extent I thought was already impossible, since I was, after all, already proportionally handicapped in this endless chasm of darkness. But then a wave of light, a body of Thought, appeared, and wrapped around me, engulfing me, appearing before my eyes in stunning reality:

I saw myself; yes, observed myself from a detached perspective, a perspective that gave me the odd sense of transcendence, as though I were a god observing man, a chess player observing his pawn, a fisher observing his bait. But these examples are not entirely accurate, for, as I observed myself standing at the edge of a plain white bed, in a plain white room, I got a strong sense that I had no control over what was going to happen, that I was suspended in a place where I had no will over my actions, as though observing myself in the future or in some other predestined act. I forgot that I must be still falling down that chasm, for the floor beneath me felt solid enough, the fluorescent lights were realistically blinding, and the me standing next to the bed looked absurdly real, every detail accounted for. As I observed myself, however, I noticed something was off. This Ishmael was clutching the side of the bed, and his shoulders were obscenely caved in, as if some force had clutched at his back and driven him downwards. His neck was bent, and a shadow of wretchedness marked his facial features, distorting his expression to that of inconceivable anguish. As I observed myself, my eyes went from my body and trailed to the bed, on which I realized someone was lying, the white blankets wrapped around in a pristine manner. The person was holding a book. And the person was Mother.

The book she was holding was instantly familiar to me, for I saw, from my omniscient gaze in the corner of the room, the gold letters on the dull green finish. It was Journey to the Center of the Earth, *and it was closed. I remember just a few days ago that there was a red bookmark in the book, more of a makeshift placeholder than anything else, but as I perceived the book that my mother was holding in this plain white bed, I noticed the absence of any such bookmark. So it was a dream, after all, a distorted version of reality that resembled my life enough for me to believe it, but with a few minor discrepancies. And so I pinched myself. Nothing happened.*

Mother laid the book gently at her linen-wrapped side, letting out an inaudible but very visible sigh. "I'm sorry Ishmael, I think that's all I can manage for now," she managed to say in a soft voice, but I could tell, even from my angle, that the effort she had given to say this much had been too great, and her head sank back into her pillow. With a faint smile, she gazed at me, the me at the edge of the bed. "Promise me you'll read it on your own."

My other self caved, finally, at this, knees buckling, hands reaching out, kneeling at the bed, tears running down. His hands clutching Mother's thin pale ones. "No, don't say that, you can read it to me later. Not today. You can read it tomorrow." Clutching hands, dreaded tears. But she sank backwards into the pillow. "You've only just started it, you can't just…"

"I know," she said, "That's why I'm sorry."

"You can't just stop now," Ishmael said again, "This is the one time you weren't busy, and—"

"Ishmael." My mother's voice simply said. "Ishmael." And Ishmael looked as though this word had sunk into his chest, had snuck like night into his little heart, as though it had ground his bones like broken glass. He clutched her hand even harder. "NO." No. That sudden answer, that unforeseen surfacing expulsion. But here, it was not a retort. It was not a fiery response. It was a cry, a cry for help, a pleading.

"I have a note for you to read later," Mother eventually said, past the sound of Ishmael's grief; and he heard it, though his head was buried into the sheets,

though he was trying to drown his sorrow in the bedding. She took out a folded red piece of paper, opened Journey to the Center of the Earth, *and placed it in the middle of the book, as though it were some sort of makeshift placeholder, much like a bookmark. "Just promise to read it tomorrow, when I'm..." she paused and looked at Ishmael's contorted features, saturated in tears. "Then I hope you'll understand."*

"No." Ishmael said again, his voice different, masked through a layer of tears, "I won't understand. I'll never understand."

"But you must." Mother said. "Take the book." And she pressed it, it and its familiar gold lettering, its familiar dull green finish, and its familiar red folded bookmark into Ishmael's unwanting hands. The view from my corner view blurred, but I could still hear Ishmael's dejected pleading, the voice of a boy who knows he's lost the fight but won't stand down, "But you promised..."

The figure of Ishmael and his mother was then enveloped by a black shroud of mist, and I lost sight of the scene. I was floating in darkness.

"You promised..."

8. THE THERAPIST

Now that I try to recall, no past nightmare had sunk into my mind as deeply as this one. No dream had ever stood out in stunning reality, no dream had threatened to hold significance. Except this nightmare. Except this nightmare, which appeared in stunning vividity and closely followed my descent into the bottomless chasm. Was it a dream within my dream of falling? Or was the falling real and my vision a mere fantastical representation of my plagued mind, the same mind that had rashly rushed at Berg with his own switchblade? Since it was obviously a nightmare, what was its purpose? Or did it have a purpose? Was it merely a trifle, an unquestioned detail that meant nothing and had no reason to exist, much like Berg telling me an alleged haunted house wasn't actually haunted, and describing every minute detail of it? Because that was the main thing, that was the most nontrivial of matters, the monster that hung above me as I dangled in the darkness of nothing: did it mean anything? Was it really, *really* a figment of the mind? Or was the vision just that — a vision? Some sort of foreknowledge?

And that thought was a monster, a monster large and frightening, looming over me. It couldn't be, couldn't be about my mother, because that would mean that…

And then a glow of light perpetrated my surroundings. The monster became real, and I could discern where the hard lines of its face began, its nose a jutting crevice of stone, its eyes a cold, glossy texture that glinted in the newly-found light as they peered down at me from their lofty perch. And then as I came slowly to my actual senses, I saw glasses on the face, and the face became a human face as it looked at me, blinked at me, the mouth formed and began to appear very much like a human mouth, hard-lined lips to complement the generally grim expression this human man wore. And then a voice emanated from the lighted scene; but the voice came from outside my peripheral field, a voice not belonging to the grim man who peered down at me, a voice I recognized, a grainy but soft voice, a voice that had been gone for so, so long, it seemed, confined in one of those city offices miles and miles away, for hours and hours every day. Dad?

"...this is what I was talking about..." Dad's voice spoke to the grim man in glasses, "...this is what he...*does*." And his voice was worried, wavering ever so slightly. Was it afraid?

"What I remember from our phone call," the glasses said, "is that this goes on for — what — hours?"

"Yes," Dad's voice replied, "He'll lay like this for...days, even...and then he'll just start...well...screaming...for hours at a time. I close the doors to his bedroom, but obviously Lizzie is scared the hell out of her mind. Can you imagine — ?"

"Well he isn't screaming now, is he?" The glasses asked tartly.

"Well, no..."

"And how long has this been going on, again?"

"About a week and a half. Really, ever since we...relocated."

"So I heard."

"Ever since..."

The glasses looked sharply at the speaker. "He's waking up now."

Reality fully came upon me.

"Why hello there, young man," the glasses patted me on the shoulder. "What's your name?"

"Who are you?" Light infiltrated my senses fully. I was lying in my bed, facing the ceiling. But it was my bed, alright, the glow was coming from my bedside lamp. I struggled quickly to prop myself up against the bed.

"My name is Dr. Levi Helsinger," the glasses said, "But you can call me Dr. Levi," Dr. Levi added. He extended his hand, and his grim features relaxed minutely. I warily shook the offered hand.

"Ishmael."

"Ah well, Ishmael," Dr. Levi replied rather warmly, "I don't suppose you'd mind talking with me for a bit this afternoon?"

"I don't suppose so." I answered.

Dr. Levi managed a look that was slightly off-putting.

"I mean, I don't mind."

"Very well, then," Dr. Levi stood, facing my father, "I don't suppose you could give us a spare moment, Liam?"

"Of course, of course," the voice still came from outside my range of vision, "Sorry," he added, "I was hurried when I called to set this up...I didn't ask about payment..."

Dr. Levi turned to my father. Now I noticed the business suit he was wearing — a comfortable grey with a bright red and green spotted tie. I blinked. "None required," Dr. Levi said, as though he were just making up his mind about it, "Consider it a charity."

"Oh," my father managed to say before he was escorted to the door by Dr. Levi, "Well...thank you, it means a lot..."

"Yes, yes, never mind," Dr. Levi abruptly closed the door. There was a silence, then a shuffling of feet that faded as my father left.

The feet faded and then there was silence. And there was Dr. Levi, sitting on the edge of a chair that had been brought into my room, just sitting and looking, those glasses resting on the edge of his long sharp nose. I managed to sit in my bed, making sure to edge as far away as possible from the scrutinous eyes.

"I'm sure you have a lot of questions," Dr. Levi said.

"Actually, I don't," I said.

"I imagine you are wondering why I am here?"

"I know why you're here."

"Inform me." Dr. Levi leaned closer on the edge of his chair. Even closer, and now I was sure he would fall off the edge. But he didn't, somehow.

"Well, I don't know who else my mom could have meant…" I began.

"Tell me," Dr. Levi leaned even closer, seemingly defying the laws of physics as he sat upon the farthest edge of the metal chair. "What did she say?"

I squirmed underneath my sheets. I didn't particularly appreciate feeling interrogated, as though I were some sort of criminal. "She said…that I would see a man…to talk to."

"Do you know what she wanted you to talk about?"

What did my mother want me to say? The words rang in my head for a second, and then I was catapulted back into a vivid virtual memory. The knife. Berg's knife, his vice of a hand, his steel eyes, the pain of the cut, and oh did the knife cut so deep, and the blood pour so red, velvet-red…Mother had suspected me for cutting my own arms, and that's what she wanted me to talk about — my alleged depression that had caused me to cut my arms. In reality, it was all Berg's fault, Berg's hand, Berg's knife. It had been him, but no one would believe me. Maybe I should try to tell Dr. Levi, though. That it wasn't my fault. He'd understand.

But no sooner had this thought entered my mind then another one replaced it. It was the knife again. But it was in my cupboard.

Planted there by Berg. Somehow. My fury, my vengeance. My hatred. My...grief? The...*NO*. The anger, my mother leaving the room, my tears of wrath, my running at Berg. But Berg was so maddeningly relaxed! And it was as though he'd expected me...he'd just been waiting there for me to come along with his knife. And then I remembered my lunge. I remembered the flash of the knife. Except it was in my hand, and Berg was the deserving, the perpetrator, the beginning of all strife, put to an end by my hand. But it was not only my hand that had killed him, but Berg's also! He'd driven the blade further, unexplainably. The blood from his chest had poured out, had flung itself upon me like tears from the sky, had poured out red, velvet-red, raspberry-red, bookmark-red... *What did my mother want me to say?* I stared at Dr. Levi. "Your guess is as good as mine."

To my relief, Dr. Levi didn't even look perplexed. He actually sighed a rather relaxed, maybe half-way bored type of sigh, as though he'd been expecting me to say this, as though it were only natural for children to be clueless as to why their parents had dropped them into therapy without explanation.

"You know," Dr. Levi said, after peering at me for a second longer, "It *is* only natural for children themselves to be clueless as to why their parents drop them into therapy...sometimes. Often the reasons are not so easy for them to see until we get the ball rolling."

"And often there's no reason...sometimes," I replied, trying to be nonchalant.

"Yes." Dr. Levi nodded once in affirmation, "Although it is extremely rare. The parent in question typically has a reason, otherwise they would not hire a therapist, which, admittedly, can come with a bit of a price tag."

"Maybe she *thought* there was a problem, when really, she misunderstood everything," I offered, trying to be as vague as possible.

Dr. Levi raised his eyebrows and wrote something in his

notebook. "So you would say that the problem — whatever that may be — lies with your mother."

"I would say that," I said.

"Ishmael," Dr. Levi said, "would you like to tell me what this problem is?"

"I dunno," I said quickly, "she's the one who started this...therapy stuff."

"And how does that make you feel, Ishmael? Her sending you to therapy without explaining why?"

Well...how did it make me feel? She hadn't asked my permission. She'd made up a story about how I'd got cuts all down the length of both my arms, she'd targeted me as the offender, and tagged me as someone with chronic depression in need of counseling. She'd done all this without saying it outright, without speaking directly to me, without asking me for the real story, the real reason I'd got cut, without giving me a chance to tell her. And even if I had told her, she wouldn't have believed me. She hadn't given me the time to believe me. She'd used to be happy with me, and tell me stories, and tuck me in at night, and turn off the light when she'd gone, but then came the time when I would tell her terrible things, things that had happened at school, the bullies, the beatings, the insults and the sneering students and teachers attempting to shut me out. She'd gone deaf to these "stories" and had sent me back, time and again. Why, even if Berg had killed me and left me on the side of the road, she would have believed I had somehow something to do with it! *How did I feel?*

Like hell? No. Words couldn't possibly begin to describe such emotions. "I don't mind, honestly." I felt like screaming. Like jumping up from my bed and strangling Dr. Levi for asking such a stupid, careless question, as though it were a ball of dirt meant for throwing around heedlessly.

I sat in my bed underneath a thin layer of sheets and stared at

Dr. Levi. Dr. Levi gazed back at me.

He was only trying to help. Was he? But how could he, even if he wanted to? He couldn't even begin to grasp the situation I was so incredibly encapsulated in. If I told him one thing, another would be discovered, the walls would cave in, and things would become even darker. Even darker.

As if that were even possible.

I looked at Dr. Levi. His face benignly gazed back at me.

"I want to go back."

"Back where?" Dr. Levi's glasses reflected the lamp, which was perched in the corner. It was the only source of light. But it was sufficient enough. Always had been. The light from the window was absent.

"To school. I want to go to school." Dr. Levi couldn't follow me to school. Could he?

There was a pause. The face with the glasses inhaled. "It's five in the evening, Ishmael."

"When is this going to be over?"

"When will what be over?"

"This...appointment."

"Oh, I'll be out of your hair in a bit, I was just wanting to ask you a few questions, is all." Dr. Levi shifted in his seat until he seemed to deem himself adequately positioned.

I sat in my bed. I felt inadequately positioned. I was waiting.

"I was just wondering, Ishmael..." Dr. Levi's glasses reflected the lamplight into my eyes. I blinked. "Do you and your mom ever...argue?"

The silence following the question was murderous. My esophagus clenched under its grip. My heart tried to drown itself in its own blood. "What?"

"Oh, you know...any fights? Squabbles? Trivial things, really..."

"No."

The glasses moved with each maddening tilt of the head. "Any unspoken things you'd like to..."

"No."

Dr. Levi nodded, as though expecting me to say this. "I believe that will wrap it up for today. Perhaps I will see you tomorrow. Would that be alright? I've already scheduled it for two in the afternoon with your...parents, actually."

I stared at him in disbelief. He couldn't possibly have...

"I'll be at school. My parents know that. And don't...therapists...do stuff once a week?"

Dr. Levi looked contemplatively at the wall behind me for a second. "I normally do appointments by week. You're right. I just didn't want to take much time with this one. Didn't want to stretch it out unnecessarily, if you know what I mean."

"I don't." I said bluntly. "And I'll be busy."

Dr. Levi's face seemed to betray...a hint of pain? Or was it sympathy? Most definitely not. "Of course. I should have asked you about your schedule first. My apologies. Unfortunately, your parents *did* schedule it, so you'll have to talk with them. It's out of my hands, at this point."

"I will." I shifted uncomfortably in my bed. He was hiding something from me. Hiding something behind those metal rimmed glasses. Hiding something he knew about me. What could he know? What *was* there to know? There was nothing, of course. I was only telling myself this. I was a terrible liar.

That night, in bed, I stared at the ceiling.

The ceiling stared back at me.

The ceiling blinked.

And then the ceiling opened its mouth and swallowed me.

There I was, falling through a chasm of darkness — again. Falling, falling, wondering when I would stop falling, knowing that it wouldn't be for a very long time. And then there were flashes of light. The flashes of light surrounded me, they blinked like the ceiling. And, like the ceiling, they swallowed me.

9. THERAPY SESSION

I lay in my bed. I lay there, and I stared at the ceiling. The white popcorn ceiling with a boring, perplexing face. The face stared back at me, but with sightless eyes. The face didn't have a nose, or a mouth, or any other defining trait other than its eyes, which didn't exist, but somehow looked at me anyway. I had been lying there for ages. More precisely, I had been lying there for half an hour, but it was half an hour too long. Mother hadn't come in. Mother had said she would come in at seven. It was seven-thirty. Mother had promised. She had promised to read me the book. But already it was a broken promise.

"Mom, can you read tonight before bed?" I would say. The dinner table had long since passed on from being communal. Dad was always at work, and my sister was playing at a friend's house, more often than not. And so the table at dinner time was a table for two; a mother and her son. The son sat at the table, staring at his untouched bowl. And the mother was at the head of the table, clumsily eating the microwavable bowl of soup, head turned to the screen of her laptop, typing. Probably typing an email. Probably trying to convince someone on the other side of the world to buy her company's office supplies. Or something boring. Her head would be turned from me. And so I would have to repeat myself to get a response. "Can you read tonight before bed?"

"Mhm, of course, after work, honey."

Honey.

"Mom, but when?"

"Soon, sweetie."

Sweetie.

"Can you read at seven?"

"Yes. Seven." Click click click.

Seven. Seven sharp. Seven on the dot. I would make sure to clean my bowl extra well. It was six-thirty now, but I would jump in my bed anyway. Waiting was fun. Waiting was enjoyable. Seven on the dot.

Click, click, click. Words were manifested, sent away, never to be seen again. What did they matter? They were just words. Words that could be typed quicker than a blink, and sent away, sent away to a foreign place. It didn't matter what they said. All that mattered was that they had been sent.

Seven o' clock. I jumped in bed. Waiting was fun.

Seven thirty. Eight. Waiting was overrated. The ceiling was staring too long, too hard. My book was too dusty, too alone.

And she didn't come.

Not that I was surprised. I had long since grown accustomed to waiting, waiting long past the seven-thirties, long past the setting of the sun. I had long since grown used to watching my book accumulate dust and stare back at me from its solitary corner in my bedroom, look at me forlornly, unblinking, alone. I had grown used to this personal mirror. Something I would look at to see myself.

Mother still hadn't come in. Probably, she was busy. Probably, she was in her room, working. Looking at the screen of her dim, lifeless computer. Probably.

Not that I was surprised.

Mother?

"Mom? When are you going to read?"

And then I realized I was in my actual room. The room with the shuttered windows and the single bedside lamp. The room with the dark brown walls and the smooth drywall ceiling. The ceiling without a face, the ceiling that didn't look back at me when I stared. I got out of my bed. I was going to school. Who cared what the students thought? Who cared what the teachers thought? And who cared what my mother thought, really?

Stabbing Berg had been a dream, after all. I had woken from this cruel event in my same old bed. It had been a dream. Deep down, in my unconscious mind, I had longed to kill him. To take his knife and give it back to him. To give the tongue of his heart a taste of his own medicine. And hopefully, in some fantasy world, Berg had felt the cool, apathetic steel cleave his skin. Hopefully he'd felt it, and from doing so, adopted an empathy no one else would ever hold for me.

Berg gone; deep down, in the cavern of my soul, I had desired this — had I not? What I had yearned for in my unconscious, that had I dreamt. Naturally. So Berg was still alive. Was I relieved? There was no time to think. My door opened. Mother?

It was the psychologist. The black wire glasses pinched his face and stood on his nose, holding up their lenses for him to peer at me through. "Ishamel, how are you?" He said in a rather congenial tone. I didn't want to hear his congeniality.

"Fine."

We were back at it. Back at the staring game, the game where Dr. Levi attempted to dig into the recesses of my soul and my eyes refused him this window. It was a rather easy game, especially when I convinced myself that I didn't have anything in my soul to be found out. Especially when I believed that my eyes were not windows in the first place. I believed I was a slab of drywall. There was nothing to see.

But Dr. Levi eventually tired of staring into my eyes, probably under the impression that I *was* outwardly nothing more than a bit of drywall, in both function and usefulness. More must be done.

Dr. Levi spoke. "Your mother tells me that you've had...some trouble in school. She's worried about you."

"Is she?" It was more of a rhetorical question, a voice of skepticism.

"How do you mean, is she?" Dr. Levi launched himself onto my rhetoric.

I flinched. I had slipped.

"Nothing. I was just...wondering. I haven't seen her in a bit, so."

"Well, you will no doubt talk to her soon; apparently, she thinks it's better if you voice any of your concerns to me right now."

There was a pause, a rather uncomfortable one. Dr. Levi leaned closer, studying me. "And of course she's worried, she's your mother, isn't she?" And then the following silence was most irritating. It pulled at the hairs of my neck, and I could feel the sweat run along the pores of my skin.

"Of course." And I avoided eye contact. Perhaps I thought that if his eyes did not look straight into mine, I could escape, if only abstractly. My peripheral vision compromised this irrational utopia.

"So how are you adjusting to school?" Dr. Levi reverted back to his opening topic, but with a slightly varied approach, as though hoping I would eventually fall prey to his use of multi-faceted semantics.

I was no one's fool. "It's alright." Alright? Yes, Ishmael. Alright is the perfect word. Alright means a great deal and nothing at all. Alright leaves room for interpretation and restricts interpretation at the same time. Alright is perfect.

"I hear that you've had some trouble with a few other students?"

I continued staring at the wall, quite aware that he was still staring directly at me. The stare all by itself threatened to bring the walls of my room closing in. I felt slightly claustrophobic.

I attempted to avoid the question by implementing another.

"When can I go back to school?"

"Berg, the school bully. At least that's what you've called him. Would you mind telling me about him?"

Berg. The world grew cold. My eyes darted to his, and I murmured a silent prayer. What did he know? What secrets had he discovered? But now it was my turn to stare in vain, staring through his eyes as though they were nothing more than a slab of drywall; they betrayed nothing. My attention had shifted at the question of Berg. This shift had not gone unnoticed.

"So you know Berg, then? Come on, Ishmael, what is he like?" The prying, the questioning, the never ending fixation.

But...*What is he like?* A question in the present tense. I breathed a sigh of relief. Maybe it was safe. Besides, Dr. Levi already knew of his existence — it would be futile to elude the acknowledgement. "Oh, he's...he's Berg. Not the brightest kid."

"Ishmael. Tell me." Dr. Levi was pleading. It wasn't all that emphatic, but it was honest. Dr. Levi really wanted to know. He really wanted to help me. Maybe he actually cared. What were the chances?

I stared at him again. "The first day he threw me on the ground. The cement, outside the classrooms. And then the next time, he did the same thing. And I wasn't able to go to school the day after that either."

"And do you mind telling me where you were injured?"

I looked at Dr. Levi for a long moment before slowly indicating the bruises and cuts on my arms, and the clotted wounds on the back of my skull. Dr. Levi took this in for another long moment.

"And the school did nothing about...this Berg, and the others?"

"No."

"And why not?"

Yes, why hadn't they, after all? Well, no one had seen it happen. It was all hearsay. He did this, he did that. But there was physical evidence. I was bruised, cut, injured. And yet...and yet. "No one cares."

There, I had said it. No one cared. They didn't, they hadn't, no one had. Berg hadn't cared. The very idea of him caring about anything was laughable. The teachers didn't care. The principal didn't care. Of all people, no, not the principal. He didn't care enough to even remember my name.

"And your parents?" Dr. Levi asked, somewhat innocently, but I knew that the question was a knife, an intentional weapon aimed for the chink in my armour. My parents. My father...well, he cared a bunch, didn't he? Maybe he didn't even know about it. Maybe Mother never mentioned it. Would it surprise me if she hadn't? Maybe it wasn't a big enough issue to bring up. Sipping on wine, late at night. Small talk. A TV show or two. Just mom and dad. How was your day? It was alright, how about you? How are the kids doing? Oh, they're doing well, in fact, I'm impressed that they've adjusted to the new place so well. And school. That's good, I'm glad to hear it.

No mention of Ishmael, perhaps? No concerns brought up about sociopathic maniacs, the psychological and physical assault? No room for that. It was an unfortunate rabbit trail. Didn't want to go down that road. Dad was too busy, he wouldn't want to have more trouble on his mind.

Had Mother been thinking this? I could only imagine. But imagination was a wild animal, and it did what it pleased. It trod a path between a dismal reality and an even more unfortunate cynicism that mirrored the perceived reality in many fundamental ways. Perhaps the two were one. Or the one was two.

So what did my parents think?

"She doesn't believe me." I said, finally. I had been considering the option of an imprisoning silence, but concluded that it would not suit me. I had been silent enough. I had locked myself away for a little longer than desirable.

"She doesn't believe you about the bullying?"

I nodded. "She makes me go back to school. And doesn't believe me."

"Have you told her about Berg."

"Yes, all of it. She thinks I'm trying to skip school."

"How does that make you feel, Ishmael?"

"Like she doesn't believe me." I knew I was cheating. This wasn't a feeling. It was a fact about my life. Maybe it didn't matter, maybe it was a feeling and a fact at the same time. But Dr. Levi, he was attentive. His attention was invested. When I had shown him the scratches and cuts on my arms, he'd nodded. When I had shown him the ghastly bruise on the back of my skull, his eyes had widened, as though it really were ghastly. I had imagined his glasses as a reflection of his soul; now I saw my folly. A person isn't what their outward characteristics make them out to be, sometimes. Sometimes there is more to a person than their accessories. Maybe, someplace, hidden far away there is empathy. Something that makes you human. Well, I felt like Dr. Levi had this something. He looked at me like no one else had. Like he actually wanted to know. Like he was actually...listening. I had not predicted it, yet somehow, inconceivably, I felt that talking to him was doing a great deal, more than I could have ever wanted or expected. But once the feeling happened, I realized I wanted it. I had a chance to be understood.

"No one really cares about what happens, it's like they're too busy with their own lives to pay attention — and Berg is the one who grabbed me, and he threw me onto the concrete, which almost killed me, and my mom's like...well, she doesn't say anything, she just looks worried, like she's worried about me. About *me*." I laughed, letting the pain in my mind seize me and spill, trying to get rid of it all, wash it out. "Like, she's not worried about school, or Berg. Actually," I leaned closer as though divesting an important piece of a mystery to Dr. Levi, "I don't think she believes that Berg exists."

Dr. Levi looked mildly surprised at this. "And why would you say that?"

"She doesn't believe anything I tell her anymore. I mean, she used to at least try to understand. She called the principal once, actually...no, it was the principal who called her. And she just listened to him, just listened to him say all those...*lies* about me, about how he's worried about *my* behavior — my behavior! And she doesn't do a thing. Doesn't lift a finger." Dr. Levi, he was listening, and his posture, countenance, and tone seemed to open a valve in a rotting heart. It was like a medical knife, cutting out an infection, and letting the diseased blood escape, bleed, pour out of the lesion. "She'd just sit there, look at me. She shakes her head, and then leaves. Like she doesn't know what to do. Why wouldn't she know what to do? If I could tell her, just make her believe...what does she think is happening? How else could this...?" I looked at my arms, the many cuts that were just healing, just beginning to scab over, the bandages. It had been days, days. I had watched as the blood thickened, as it self-perpetuated its cleansing, as my body adapted and healed. My outside injuries were healing, and yet my heart felt as though it had just been torn open again.

Dr. Levi nodded solemnly. "Ishmael, if you could tell your mom one thing...would it be that you want her to believe you? That you want her to take the time to listen to your feelings?"

The time to listen. The time to...be there. Sit beside me a while longer, maybe believe me for once. Maybe she could read two chapters, instead of just one. This alternative was the other side of the line, the other side of reality, a place where there was no dull grey, where I felt peace and security, where I felt like I had a home. But it was just that: on the other side of the line. Something unreal. Something searched for without having reason for its existence. My gaze dropped to the solid white bed sheets that wrapped around me in a disorderly and whimsical fashion. I shook my head slowly.

"No."

"What do you mean?"

"It doesn't matter."

"What doesn't matter?"

As I spoke the last remaining energy I had to sit up left me, and my words leached into the air, staining the paper ambience like molasses.

"It wouldn't matter if she listened, she could listen to my feelings all day. And it wouldn't make a difference. Because she just doesn't care. At all. About me."

Why did the simpleness of the answer sting as sharp as a needle, why did it drain the life out of me? Was this what truth was? Was this how it felt? Was this what the blind man experienced when he opened his eyes for the first time, when he saw the world for what it truly was, and found that it had been dark all along? Was this the emotional high one gets when one finally lands on the answer that they've been searching for their whole lives, only to find that it is a dark tunnel with many twists and turns, all roads leading to a dead end? Was this what a dream feels like when you wake? Was this me staring into the universe, looking for comfort, and then the universe staring coldly back? Was it better that way?

I thought she'd been there for me. I thought she'd been like a mother. I thought she had actually cared. But I had known all along, hadn't I? Her reading to me was only a distraction, a facade. Look, Ishmael, your mother reads to you. She's spending time with you. So she must care about you. I had created this interpretation in my mind. But I couldn't let go now. Where would that land me? I must hold on a little longer. Must I hold on to my creation?

My head sank back into my pillow as the first convulsion of grief ripped at my lungs, yanked at my chest, wracked my throat.

Clenching, unclenching. It was like the rain. The sky seemed to open its gates and out poured the water, soaking, pouring, submerging my world in a blanket of darkness. It went on like this until my room was dark, and no light came through the window, or from my lamp. A little while later, I found my pillow soaked with tears, and my face wet. There had been no rain.

10. THE WARNING

I stared at my ceiling, that canvas, that pathway to a separate universe. I tried to paint the oceans and the sand in my mind, recreate that world once again; I reached to hear the sound of her voice, her words come to life, and paint it on that canvas. Could I escape again? I wanted to follow Jules Verne into the center of the earth, leave my present darkness far behind me, and uncover my memories of light. I knew they were there, somewhere. But I had lost them. Could I do that? But who was I asking? I wanted to look past the conflict, look past her shunning, shun these remembrances, and if my will proved strong enough, erase them, make them as though they never happened. They weren't real, it didn't explain anything. Mother had always sympathized with me, spent time with me, read to me, time and time again. Where were those memories? Now she was cold and distant, and uncaring. Without love. This wasn't like her, somehow it was all a bad dream.

Please, can I wake up now?

Who was I asking?

Maybe once I answered that question I could answer many more. Whatever it was, I felt myself sinking away from the ceiling. Panic drenched me as I felt my body stretch away from my comfort, falling backwards, into my bed, leaving my bed behind, falling.

Hello, chasm. How infinite and powerful you are. Please stop.

And yet. The chasm greeted me, and didn't stop. I kept falling. Dark. Light.

Dark. And finally Light.

I watch myself sitting on a couch. I guess we get a couch at some point in the future. The living room is large, with polished wood floors, and high hung chandeliers reflecting ambient light through celestial glass. So maybe it's a friend's house. Or a relative's house. My future self sits on the couch, with mud caking his shoes. Ishmael looks at the mud on his shoes. He looks and looks. His face is wet, his eyes are red and puffy. His hair is topsy turvy. He looks like he just came back from fishing. Or sailing.

But there's mud on his shoes.

A thought enters my omniscient observing mind. It's Berg. Berg's still preying on me. How did I last this long? Maybe it's next week, or a month from now. Or a year. And Berg's still beating Ishmael up. Still having his bit of fun. And here I watch as Ishmael sits, crying, with mud on his shoes. It makes sense. And yet it doesn't. It couldn't be Berg; Ishmael is not marred with cuts or bruises. He does not appear to be at his own home. It must be some occasion.

There's mud on his shoes.

Then Father walks through the front door, with the same disheveled appearance. He's holding an umbrella. He's wearing formal clothing. A large group files in behind him, their footsteps marking the atmosphere, their murmurs infiltrating the sacred silence. They all match in appearance. They are all wet. And there's mud on their shoes. I look out the window. The sky is clouded over and the Earth outside looks wet and wounded with craters of water. And there's a trail of footsteps running across the front yard, running away, and coming back, vanishing in the distance, and leading all the way to the front door, muddied imprints of the near past, a blueprint of what has just occurred.

Father sits beside Ishmael, just sitting there with him, sharing the silence. He stares at the mud on his own shoes, and allows the time to progress as it will.

Ishmael makes no movement, shows no acknowledgment of his Father's presence. To him the only thing that exists seems to be the mud on his shoes. Oh, and now he's looking at his hands, his shaking hands, hands that are uncontrollable, that defy composure, that shake and writhe. And they're covered in mud.

I move my other-worldly being through the door, leaving myself and my father behind me, leaving behind the somber commune, and walk outside. The rain surges around me, passing through me as I walk. I follow the trail, the clues, the footsteps, the imprints that run all together in a hopeless mess. I know Ishmael's footprints are among the disarray, and so I follow them.

The path takes me through the front yard. The grass is bent over, burdened with rain droplets. The frail trees cower as the wind reaches at them. I see the wind, but the wind passes through me, as though I am not here. And it is because I am not. I am merely observing something. I do not know what that something is yet. But I know that the imprints in the mud will lead me to whatever it is soon enough. Then I will know why I am here. Is it really that simple? Can a literal mud path reveal a metaphysical destiny? Who am I asking?

The path leads me past the burdened grass stalks, leads me away from the cowering trees. The path stretches onward, runs along the Earth in a haphazard fashion, seemingly never ending. Yet I continue to follow it. I have nothing left to do, after all. And, I hope, something reasonable awaits. Something that answers questions. I can only hope. The trail goes on and on. Did I mention this? How it stretches onward, seemingly never ending? Perhaps I just did. Perhaps I didn't. Time passes quickly. Or doesn't pass at all. Or doesn't exist. How would I know? I am only walking down a mud path, searching for something. Nothing else has to exist. If it does, then it merely does, and I do not care.

Nevertheless, I do arrive somewhere. Eventually I reach a place where the mud path ends and a stone one begins. The place where the stone path begins is ornamented with a large iron gate, broken by an arch in the middle. It towers above me and almost stares down at me, daring me to pass through. Is this where my future self walked? I see how the footsteps beneath my feet run along and collide confusedly with the stone path, and break off there. And so logically, they continue, though unseen, along the stone. And so I follow. I don't have anything left to do, remember? Or maybe I do, but I am unaware. Such things have happened to people, I believe. I walk along this stone path, searching for familiarity, something of interest, something that is supposed to mean something.

I search for, and I find. As I walk, I am greeted by large stones, which are placed uniformly in the ground. They are polished in perfect geometrical shapes. There are words on them. These words are too small for me to care. I pass by. And I look, look for something particular. I don't know what it is until I see it. A splash of color. Directly ahead, there's a special-looking stone with words. Its specialness is not derived from the shape, or the polish. It is not derived from the fancy lettering, or the placement. Rather, it is singular in its feeling. Feeling? Did I just describe a stone as having feeling? How else can I describe it? It perches along others, and yet it looks alone, and calls to me. The other singularity is the flowers. No other stone has these particular flowers. Just this stone. And the flowers are bright red, unwilted, almost cheerful. And yet as I listen, I hear the sound they're making. The sound of sobbing, as though the flowers are crying. Somehow they are trembling, writhing in an unspeakable pain. I approach the stone with the letters. I look at the earth at the foot of the stone, and see it pushed around, muddled, dug out, by what seems to be the work of human hands. The mud forms a fresh hole in which I see broken grass, dirt and rain. They are mixed about, distorted with dampness, compounded. But in this mudhole, mixed about with the dirt and the grass and the wetness, yet also starkly distinct in color and form, I behold a pile of broken pieces of paper. The paper is red and bright, and it is torn. Torn into little pieces and thrown into the hole with the mud. They have just been thrown in a moment ago, and they are just beginning to cave in to the rain, wilting before my eyes, and becoming one with the dirt, now almost indistinguishable. I kneel beside the weeping flowers, the flowers that are somehow capable of such emotion, beside the hole in the ground with the torn pieces of paper, and read the letters graven onto the stone. Then I feel like the flowers, blood-red, anguished. I feel like the red paper, torn and drenched with unspeakable pain.

The uncontrollable spasms overtake me. My lungs clench and unclench. I open my mouth and scream into the ground. I scream and scream until I can't anymore. And then the clouds above me open up and it's like the rain, again. It's like the night closes in, and there's darkness, and there's nothing to support me. And then the tears run down like the rain, and saturate the world in my unexplainable existence.

Just as soon as it had leapt upon me, the prophecy fades before my eyes and leaves me to my present darkness.

I had thought it might happen, somehow. Figured it had been more than a dream. First it had been Mother in a white bed, face carved with fatigue and life's inevitability. Then it had been her name carved into stone. How did I know, though—that it wasn't a dream? Maybe it was a coincidental sequence of dreams, amplifying my inner animosity that pre-existed towards my mother. That would explain it. That's what dreams are, right? Distorted representations of our soul, to an extent. But something was different about these dreams. Dreams may represent my innate consciousness, but my innate consciousness was telling me that they were less like dreams, and more like someone was trying to tell me something. Or I was trying to tell myself something. How does that work? If I am really trying to communicate with myself, then which part is it that is talking, and which part is listening? Do I need to know? Would it make a difference? In either case, I knew somehow they weren't dreams. Somehow I was being told something of grave importance. It was a task. My task. And I had to do something about it.

Maybe I now had to try saving her. Try to save my mother. Attempt to bridge the space, attempt to tell her about my visions, what would happen, try to fix all of it. Change the future. Perhaps this was how it was done — getting back to her, reclaiming what we once had, that closeness. No, it was laughable. She hadn't believed me about school

— why would she believe me about these visions? Hey mom, I had these weird dreams about you dying. But they aren't dreams, they're trying to tell me that in the future you're going to die! We have to do something to keep it from happening!

No. This was ludicrous. Was it? Or was I supposed to do it? Or both? Maybe I could fix this without telling her. Fix what? All I knew was that she was going to die of some illness, after being confined in a hospital. It was all so vague — how would I fix what I didn't know? Cancer? Blood poisoning? A slow-killing virus? Years of depression? What clues did I have to go off of? Why did I have mud on my hands in the vision? The hole in the ground, of course. Why had I dug the hole? What were those torn pieces of paper? If I could go back to that moment, perhaps I could piece them back together, like a puzzle, to discern the whole. Figure out what they meant.

It didn't matter, the answers to these questions didn't matter. The fact remained, I must do something. Or tell someone. But who would listen? Who would actually care?

11. Try to remember

"How are you today Ishmael?" Dr. Levi began as usual.

"You have to listen."

"I have always listened, Ishmael."

"You need to help me, you need to help my mom."

Dr. Levi looked at me intently. "What is on your mind, exactly?"

I spoke in a low voice. "Something terrible is going to happen."

Dr. Levi continued looking intently, hardly moving at the point. His expression was incredulous, as though he had been searching for gold and had stumbled upon diamonds. Had he been searching for this, though? Did he know, too…? Did he have these same visions? Is this why he was helping me? Why he was meeting so often, more than I could understand, why he was so concerned about me and my mother? Maybe he could help me, after all, now that he understood. But the moment was gone. His intent expression loosened, and his shoulders gave away the minute suggestion of defeat, his posture like a deflating balloon. I couldn't — couldn't look into his eyes, now that there was pity in them, now that he was shaking his head slowly, letting the hint of a sigh escape his mouth. Now he shifted in his seat, inching a little closer to me, and the glasses shimmered, and glinted into my eyes, catching my attention although I yearned to escape. Can I leave now?

Dr. Levi spoke slowly. Deliberately. Every word was the sharp point of a knife.

"Something terrible has already happened, Ishmael. And you must try to remember."

To remember.

And then the temperature of the room fell ten degrees. And then there was denial. "What do you mean, something has already happened?" I fired back. Maybe if I kept talking I could shed the fear, swim the surface of the unforgiving ocean that threatened to drown me. "Do you mean what Berg did to me? Or maybe what my mother does, or doesn't do? How she doesn't believe me? Or maybe what school is doing to me every day? Or do you mean how depressed I've been, how I wish I could stop time, or just stop living altogether to escape it? How I want to get out of here?" And *here* meant something altogether more general than I had ever consciously realized. There was a fire, a fire that had begun ever since Dr. Levi had made an allusion to something in the past, something terrible that I was trying to hide. It had been eating at me. Now I must expel it forever. I sat up straighter. I must pretend that nothing had happened, that I wasn't thinking too hard about Berg. But my voice had a ring of fury to it, a venom laced in its controlled volume. "Can I go back to school now?"

"Why do you keep asking to go back to school?" Dr. Levi immediately responded, "You've been attacked every time you go there. According to your stories, you have."

Stories. There it was again. So that was it. They were just stories, to Dr. Levi. He was no different than my mom. Or the principal.

"Surely you don't want to go back until Berg is gone." He said.

"I don't care."

"No, maybe not anymore." Dr. Levi held a slow but heavily calculated tone in return, measuring my mind with his piercing eyes. "You know why, I think."

I threw my sheets off of my quivering body. The temperature was rising, and I felt that fire burning hotter, felt that seething rising up again.

Dr. Levi didn't betray any sign of alarm, but continued in that same calculated tone, "And of course, you won't be able to return to school, probably not for a very long time, if ever. You know why, but I can tell you're hiding it."

But I couldn't hide it, could I?

"Yes, I killed that idiot!" I yelled, my vocal chords straining at the channeled energy surging through him. "And he had it coming! He had it coming for a long time! Is that what you wanted to hear? Wait, no, it gets better. I used his own knife — the same one. He cut me, but I cut him — and he had it coming. He had it coming for a long time. Someone had to do it. I had to do it! I had to." Suddenly my energy was gone. Inexplicably drained. I fell back onto my sweat-stained pillow. "I had to." My breath came in short gasps. I stared at the ceiling, praying for the chasm to swallow me where I lay. "I had to do it."

Dr. Levi took this all in without the slightest apparent surprise or alarm. He just looked at me, looked at me like he always had, behind his metal wireframes, perceiving everything and remaining impassive. "Really, Ishmael, you do yourself an injustice." How could he banter like he did? Throw about these comments with such flippancy? "You didn't use Berg's knife." He pulled out that shiny metal blade, took it out like it was a mere trinket, and placed it on the table. I pulled away from it, scrambling in my sheets to press myself against the back of the bed. It couldn't be...how....?

"No."

"No what?"

"That's not mine. I never had...it was Berg..."

Dr. Levi's eyes flickered. "Oh, no. No no no. This is yours. It's yours, Ishmael. Don't you recognize it?" I stared at Dr. Levi, as he held that shiny metal blade in front of my eyes. His brow darkened as his eyes narrowed. The next question he asked caught me unawares. "Do you know why you moved to the city, Ishmael?" I stared at him. I shook my head. Then I shook my head again, thinking, my brain muddied and deluded. I couldn't...I couldn't...I mustn't...I couldn't remember. For my dad to find a job? Dr. Levi sighed, rather dismissively. Then he did something altogether extraordinary. He reached one of his long arms towards me but past me, landing instead on my precious book, Journey to the Centre of the Earth. He twisted his fingers around my red paper bookmark and pulled in one short spasm. The red paper flew out, grasped in his outstretched hand, as he held it in front of my surprised countenance. Now I saw for the first time how makeshift of a bookmark it was, with one side of it forming a grotesquely jagged edge, as though the majority of the red paper had been torn off, torn into little pieces, torn into little pieces of red and thrown somewhere, somewhere with dirt and water, thrown away. He was holding the survivor, that one remnant. The one I'd kept this whole time, tucked away in my book. That one red piece of paper.

"You must try to remember."

PART II

The Other Part

1. Mother?

I lay in my bed and looked at a pale blue wall. My bed was beyond my initial recognition, as was the soft pale blue of the wall surrounding me, and yet the image of both together produced an undeniable sense of remembrance: the house, the house with the nice interior and the blue walls. It was the house of my future visions. The house where it all happened. My dreams, the prophecies, all led here. I'd had flashes of this place before, but only once I'd fallen into some chasm of sorts. Now I was seeing it with much more reality: the future.

"Mother?"

There was no reply, and the sheets stretched around me as I pulled myself up to a seated position. There was only silence. I heard small footsteps enter the kitchen and the pantry door open. I heard the crunch and rustle of a cereal box being opened. My little sister. I jumped to the ground and entered the dining room as fast as I thought likely, but already her mouth was full of Hello Kitty Cheerios. I sighed inwardly.

"Where's mom?"

She looked at me for a second, chewing. "I dunno." Between swallows. "Work?"

Of course. She could be at another "meeting." Either that or shopping. She seemed to do little else. And yet the pantry, I noticed, had continued to decline in its previous stores of food.

"Why?" Chewing. Crunch crunch crunching. Swallowing.

"Never mind." I turned and walked back to my room. It was seven o' clock. Seven in the evening.

She had said that she would read. She had promised. But I shouldn't have been surprised. And yet here I was, surprised again. One of those melancholy surprises that you'd secretly hoped wouldn't happen, a spark of hope you let get the better of you. But I shouldn't have been even remotely taken aback. This cycle had started a year before, one long bone-grinding year before. The broken promises. The distance.

The table had been furnished that morning, that morning one year before. I sat at the table, and she chugged her coffee down with an effort. Her eyes were more bloodshot than usual. Her hair was done poorly. I was just now noticing this — was it new?

"Mom, tonight, remember you said you'd read…?"

She didn't look up. "Mhm, yes sweetie." Sweetie. The keyboard on her laptop pattered in a random crescendo. Something about her…it was new. And it was different. A tired sort of trail that a wisp of her hair made behind her ears. I hadn't noticed until today. She hadn't put on makeup yet either. Oh well, sometimes she did, sometimes she didn't. But still. Something…it was…elusive, what was I trying to think of? It was so…not like yesterday?

"Your mom's just been working harder around this time of the year," my dad had explained that night, the year before, in my dream. He explained this to me at ten. Ten at night. My books were sprawled out across my bed in a haphazard fashion, so that one might have assumed that a miniature dust devil had recently visited bedroom space, and thrown it all about.

"Work's been real rough on me, and I'm sorry, Ishmael." My mother said vaguely behind her laptop screen the next morning, a year before. A year before when her makeup had stopped making it correctly on her face, or not making it on there at all. A year ago when her hair stopped being perfectly combed and pulled back, a year ago: the beginning of broken promises. Of fear.

"Tonight, then?" Not tonight, probably not this week, she told me. But you said...you said...I would plead and bargain. Then I would wait a whole week. A whole week where I read, entertaining myself in my bedroom till the night slipped in and shut my eyes. A whole week where it was just me and my school and my books. A whole week where I would listen at my mother's bedroom door in the early morning, wondering why I was so earnest, why I was so constantly there, and then feeling my heart beat normally once again when I heard her moving about in the little area outside my sight, outside of my world.

And then, after a week had passed, I would ask again. "Can you read? Remember that book we started last year, the *Journey to the Centre of the Earth?* The one by..."

"Of course, sweetie."

"Seven o' clock?"

"That should work."

Seven, seven on the dot. I would jump into bed at six thirty just to be sure. I would wait until seven. Then I would wait after seven. I would wait until seven thirty, begging my ears to give even the illusion of the sound of her footsteps, to hear the sound of the doorknob turning, beseeching my eyes to hallucinate her shadow falling across my door frame. Each week I would fall asleep to tears, and wake many times in the night to find my pillowcase saturated.

The morning afterwards. "You said, you promised..."

"No, I didn't promise, Ishmael." No. *No.* How I had grown to hate that word. But this hatred had started that year ago, that long, tedious year ago. When everything changed. No. "I *am* sorry, Ishmael" my mother would say, though she knew I didn't believe her. If she was sorry, why didn't she keep her word? If she was sorry, why didn't she make it up to me? "Work has been extra crazy recently, and…"

"When will it stop being crazy?" I interjected. When?

This question appeared to have caught my mother by surprise. She looked up from her laptop screen and stared at me for a good two seconds — the longest she had for two weeks. But then the gaze was broken, and her eyes fell to her laptop screen again. Her fingers flew and the keyboard grated out an incongruous symphony. She spoke in a softer voice. "I don't know, but hopefully soon."

Hopefully soon. I could only cry at night and live in the daytime.

Starting that year ago, though my mother lived in our house, I would find myself wondering why she had left us. For that's what it seemed like, at least. It was like a ghost of someone I used to know inhabited my thoughts and typed away at the keyboard in the morning, and faded away during the evenings and into the night. That cycle repeated, and continued to repeat itself till the present. The Now of my visions:

2. SHE PROMISED

My sister's cereal munching lost its volume as I walked back to my bed, and threw myself over my covers. I winced as I landed on a pile of books. Idiot, I thought. I should have remembered I left a pile of books on my bed. They'd been waiting. And it was seven o' five. So there was still a chance...Mother was only five minutes late. I pulled the first book off the pile. *Journey to the Centre of the Earth.* I searched and finally found that I had folded one of the pages for lack of a better bookmark. It marked where we'd left off, two years ago. And for two years, I'd been waiting for my mother to finish it with me. We were only fifty pages in. The appearance of neglect did not feign itself on this book; rather, the book looked like the day I had bought it from the library bookstore, with its shiny hardcover and glistening paper edges. It was seven ten. The same routine, the same absence. But this time, she'd *promised*...this time, she'd stopped her insanely fast typing, looked me in the eye and said those words: "seven o' clock tonight, Ishmael." Seven. Tonight? I just wanted to be sure. Promise? "I promise." She'd said. She had promised. It had to mean...

I heard the front door open at long last. Seven thirty. I sprang from my bed, and my mattress bounced excitedly as I landed on the carpet and flew down the hall. As I rounded the corner leading to the kitchen and front door, I stopped short at the sight of my father, himself looking especially more worn out than usual. Bags under his eyes, his shoulders drooping like a wet piece of paper. Rain season must have already begun. His coat was damp and water droplets clung to his briefcase as he set it down heavily on the floor.

That night, we sat around our spacious fireplace, the three of us, my father, sister, and I. And that's when he told us we were selling the house.

"We're...what?" Was all I could fathom at the moment. The world seemed to blink at me and spin before my eyes. I clung to the edge of the couch. Why? Why would we...how could we? What would we do, where would we go?

"One stream of income isn't enough to support the mortgage, and all, so I thought it best that..."

"Wait." I struggled upwards, blinking repeatedly, trying to blink the reality into focus. "You said..." he said... "you said...one stream of income? Did you lose your job?"

My father looked discontented that this had slipped from his mouth, and he grimaced before speaking slowly. "Your mother actually just lost her job, economy and all, so it's been hard on her, she doesn't know what to do, and..."

"Dad." I spoke, afraid of myself, afraid of what I might find. "Where's mom?"

"Probably shopping...?"

"Why don't you text her?"

"Ishmael, calm down. Your mother usually comes back late."

"She promised she'd read...?"

My dad tried to slow the rising storm. "That was before she lost her job, Ishmael...you must understand..."

But he couldn't hold back this storm, not on his life. Now I'd put all the puzzle pieces into place, I'd called to mind that fateful day, a year ago from now, when my mother had begun to show signs of slipping away, slipping psychologically and physically from my life. "It's been a year, hasn't it, dad?" My voice rising.

My father looked frightened. Of course, it wasn't me. It was what I had said that had struck a soft place, overturned a log full of termites. He stood suddenly. "Lizzie, I think it's bedtime now, why don't you run along and get ready." My sister looked at both of us, a little shaken, and hurried out of the room. "It's been a year, hasn't it?" I repeated. I looked down to find my hands shaking uncontrollably.

"A year...what do you mean, Ishmael?" My father tried to remain calm but I could tell by the nervous movement of his hands and the fidgeting of his shoulders as he sat back down that he was afraid of what I might say next, although he knew, of course; known all along.

I didn't care about my volume anymore. I stopped clutching the couch and stood. "She lost her job a year ago, didn't she?" I shouted, my voice filling the enormous living room and bouncing off the ornately decorated walls, shaking the chandelier above me. The glass in the chandelier quivered and spun blades of light across the room. The fireplace spat and sizzled. "Didn't she?"

My father opened his mouth hesitantly and then looked at the ground.

"And you knew." My head refused to stay upright, it teetered sporadically downwards, and my mouth coagulated into a grimacing shape. "You knew all along. And my mom knew too. This whole time. She *knew.*"

"Ishmael, there's nothing to worry about, soon she'll..."

"Soon? Maybe? Possibly? Just tell me, stop *lying.*" My blunt words seemed to slap my father across the face. But when he rose to his feet and looked me in the eye...I didn't find anger, rage, frustration. I found agony, uncontrollable anguish.

"Ishmael, I didn't want to tell you."

"Just tell me!"

Then the barriers broke down, and my father's voice took its turn filling the room and sweeping upon me like an ice-cold breeze. "Your mother is sick, okay? And the doctors, they don't know...they don't know...they gave her a week today. A week at the most. I wanted to tell you, but..."

Now his voice was droning and I didn't hear much past that. Something about a hospital. And quitting work. And remedies. And her nightly excursions, trips to find experimental treatments. Which was why she was always late to come home. Why she was never here when she'd promised... I was frozen to my core, my feet fastened in place, my head pounding with my heart. His words cut through me, went straight through my skin and pinned me against an invisible wall. Only my mouth moved, groping for formations of words, tediously piecing together the painful syllables.

"*Why didn't you...tell me?*"

"Ishmael, I didn't think now was the best time..."

"*The best time?*" I spat, my chest shaking, salty water collecting around the corners of my mouth, dripping down my face. "She promised me...that she would...that she....SHE PROMISED!"

I turned and ran.

3. RED BOOKMARK

The light of the hospital flooded me. White is the color of purity. I think this is because all the colors together make white. So there's something transcendent about it, something overarching and inherent in white to all things. It's more than just the concept of all coming together to produce white. *From* white issues forth every other color, it's the starting point, the point from which all others originate. The white atmosphere of the hospital corridors bespoke a stunning purity, a purity I could not reconcile with all the grief it contained. Perhaps it was a mask, a cunning facade manufactured to paint over the muddled canvas of humanity's corruption. The world was not pure white, and so the inside of this hospital was a lie. It was all a lie to cover up the evil truth, just like the lie my mother had told me every week for an entire year to cover up the ugly reality. Why must she lie? Why must we lie? Why must one conceal the very infrastructure of the inevitable? Is it some attempt made in good faith, in the strong belief that lying changes reality, or is the lie told in deliberation, out of sheer desperation? But that had to be what it was, the desperation, the grasping for happiness and not being able to find it. It is the losing of joy that causes us to become vile, to fill the dishonest world with even more of its own joylessness. It is this endless cycle that threatens to drag us all down into the pit.

Now I heard the words "She's ready for you now," and a man in white appeared from a door in the hall. My father, Lizzie, and I walked into the room, and I was greeted by a stunningly white formation: my mother lying in bed with something like a white pillow case wrapped around her head. A faint smile played across her features, and she lay swathed in pure white bedsheets. I couldn't do this, I knew what was happening. I had seen this somewhere. In my flashes of light, my prophetic dreams. Everything played out exactly, in the perfect formation of a dream replayed. I hunched over my mother's bed, burdened by grief, my shoulders hunched awkwardly, as though a great weight hung from my neck, choking my throat, wringing wetness from my eyes.

"Where were you?" My breath came out small, my voice almost inaudible.

"Here." She mouthed more than spoke, her eyebrows knitted in concern, gazing at me. Then she saw what I was holding, clutching in my hands. The *Journey to the Centre of the Earth*.

"You promised you would…"

"Ishmael, now's not the time…" my father began, but he was cut short as my mother reached out her arm and took the book. She took it with what seemed to be her last strength, and opened it, opened it to the part where'd we left off, where I'd marked it by folding the corner of the paper. But she could only get out a few sentences. I struggled inwardly, watching her mouth move tediously, forming the words and bringing them to light. But at last it seemed too much.

Mother laid the book gently at her linen-wrapped side, letting out an inaudible but very visible sigh. "I'm sorry Ishmael, I think that's all I can manage for now," she managed to say in a soft voice, but I could tell that the effort she had given to say this much had been too great, and her head sank back into her pillow. With a faint smile, she gazed at me as I stood at the edge of her bed. "Promise me you'll read it on your own."

My shoulders caved, finally, at this, knees buckling, as my hands reached out, and I kneeled at the bed, tears running down. My hands clutched Mother's thin pale ones. "No, don't say that, you'll read it to me later. Not today. You can read it tomorrow." Clutching hands, dreaded tears. "You've only just started it, you can't just…"

But she sank backwards into the pillow. "I know," she said, "That's why I'm sorry."

"You can't just stop now," I said again, "This is the one time you weren't busy, and—"

"Ishmael." My mother's voice simply said. "Ishmael." And then this word sunk into my chest, snuck like night into my little heart, felt as though it was grinding my bones like broken glass. I clutched her hand even harder. "NO." No. That sudden answer, that unforeseen surfacing expulsion. But here, it was not a retort. It was not a fiery response. It was a cry, a cry for help, a pleading.

"I have a note for you to read later," Mother eventually said, past the sound of my grief; and I heard her, though my head was buried into the sheets, though I was trying to drown my sorrow in the bedding. She took out a folded red piece of paper, opened Journey to the Center of the Earth, and placed it in the middle of the book, as though it were some sort of makeshift placeholder, much like a bookmark. "Just promise to read it tomorrow, when I'm…" she paused and looked at my contorted face, saturated in tears. "Then I hope you'll understand."

"No." I said again, my voice was different, masked through a layer of tears, "I won't understand. I'll never understand."

"But you must." Mother said. "Take the book." And she pressed it, it and its familiar gold lettering, its familiar dull green finish, and its familiar red folded bookmark into my unwanting hands.

"But you promised..."

4. THE NOTE

But she'd promised. She'd told me she'd be there at seven. Now she was gone forever. She'd left me. And she'd lied, made me believe she would stay. The light from my lamp was cold and grey. It pinched my eyes, and slid across the desolate carpet, seeking escape. It found none. The light crept up the walls and attempted to slide through the crevices in my window, but the shutters barred its path. The rejected luminescence threw itself at my ceiling, forming mangled shadows that glowered at me.

I heard the rain drench the outside world in misery, and through the noise, I heard the doorbell. Then I heard my father's voice call up to me. It was time. It would be the last day I would sleep in this room before we moved — what better day to have a funeral? Surely there is never a better day. It is always the worst day. Father said we'd move somewhere a lot different. He said we'd go to the city, and that I would like it there, and that I would enjoy going to a new school. He said the change would be good for me. But today I would not see the city; I would be attending a funeral. My eyes fell once again on my book, and the unopened bookmark letter inside it. The red paper caught my eye, and I breathed deeply before finally pulling it out of the book. The back of it was written over with tiny lettering, so precise and so faint. But I could read it, barely:

"Ishmael, I will never forgive myself for breaking my promise. But I hope you forgive me. I know I lied to you for a while. I know I made you believe I would be returning that night, and the many nights before. I know now that it was wrong of me to make promises I could not keep. But I want you to know that I didn't lie to you because I didn't care about you, but rather, because I care deeply about you. And I felt that I could protect you by hiding the truth. I know it sounds foolish, but I actually did believe that. My greatest regret is that I did not spend as much time with you as I could have. I did not know that my time with you would be so short. Know that I will only love and adore you. Love, mom."

Before I could reach the last line, my vision blurred and the paper became splotched with tears as they flowed incessantly, without warning. I couldn't look at the note, I couldn't face what it meant: that she was really gone. I couldn't believe that, because that would mean that it was final. That what was broken could never be fixed. It was lost forever. There could be no redemption. I wept for five minutes with the red paper clutched in my fists. Then I tore it in two. I crumpled the one side with the letter on it, and stuffed it in my pocket. I put the blank part of the paper back in my book. It would serve as a reminder — not of her death, but of her life. The letter I must get rid of. I couldn't look at it, couldn't be reminded of the broken promises, the lies. Not even if there was an apology. It meant nothing to me. I must get rid of it.

My door opened and there stood my father, a deflated shadow of a man, with a sorrowful smile and a folded umbrella. It was time. I stood and left my room. I didn't turn to say goodbye.

PART III

The Final Part

1. NO ANSWER

I found myself once again in my bed. In our apartment, with Dr. Levi looking at me intently. I had been talking this whole time. I don't know exactly what I'd been saying, but he'd been listening.

"So you keep having this dream...about a funeral?"

"Yes."

"Who was this funeral for, again?"

I looked at Dr. Levi. I remembered how I'd shredded that red piece of paper with the words on it. The memory was so vague now, even though I'd had it so recently. I couldn't even remember who's words they were, who'd written it, or what they said. I only knew I had to forget. "My mom."

Dr. Levi stared unblinkingly. "And when is this funeral supposed to happen, do you think?"

"I don't know," I replied irritably. "It's sometime in the future. How am I supposed to know?"

"And you're convinced this is some kind of prophecy, a warning of sorts?"

"Yes...I don't know. It just seems too odd to be a random dream. Something that I'm supposed to know."

"And you feel like you should warn your mother...or do something to stop it from happening?"

"What else should I do? Just do nothing?"

I noticed the bright red. I didn't quite remember where I'd seen it last...I had remembered just a moment before, but already these remembrances of the past had slipped my mind as quickly as they'd come. Dr. Levi noticed I was looking at the torn piece of paper in his hand. "So do you remember, now?"

"Remember what?" I asked.

"Do you remember what this is?" Dr. Levi asked me rather pointedly.

"Um, no." I responded, somewhat vexed. "It's a piece of paper...a bookmark."

"Why is it torn?"

I shifted in my bed, wondering why I felt so uncomfortable at the question. "I don't know. My mom uses it as a bookmark, so I know where she left off."

"Do you remember why you moved here, Ishmael?" It was an out of the blue question; perhaps he thought it would catch me off guard.

"My dad got a good job offer here."

"And your mom…?"

"She doesn't work."

Dr. Levi had apparently finished asking me questions. He stood for the first time that day, leaning against his chair and just staring at me for a good while. I avoided eye contact somehow. Dr. Levi removed his glasses and rubbed his eyes, fighting back drowsiness.

"I'll see you tomorrow, Ishmael." He said with a concerning finality, and turned to leave. I called out before he could vanish through the door.

"What's going to happen about...Berg?" I asked.

Dr. Levi turned, leaning against the doorframe. He cleared his throat. "Nothing, Ishmael. Nothing at all." I wanted to ask why, but couldn't bring myself to open my mouth. But he answered before I could speak. "I contacted the school and there are no students by the name of Berg. Also, there have been no reported stabbings on the campus. I didn't want to tell you yet...or else you might think that I think you're going insane."

I stared at him. I opened my mouth. "But Berg...he did this to me…" I held my arms out. No. I couldn't have another person like my mother, someone who wouldn't believe me. I had the evidence. It was all there. Why couldn't he see it? "He literally cut my arms...they were bleeding, how else…"

"Goodbye Ishmael." Dr. Levi turned to leave again.

"Wait!" I called again from my bed. Dr. Levi stopped again, halfheartedly turning around to face me. "Can you get my mom? She said she'd read to me tonight, and it's almost seven."

Dr. Levi didn't answer. At my question, his features assumed once more the look of finality, the glazed look of one who has just finished a lengthy book and is pausing to consider the end. Perhaps this was the most horrifying thing he could have done, the worst thing that could have possibly ever happened. I didn't know why, I just felt my blood go cold, and my heart rate rise. It was a simple question, a mere request. But Dr. Levi just sighed. Then he turned and walked out. I heard his footsteps fade as he traversed the hall. I heard the front door shut. Then I heard silence. Mother?

2. SHE'S WAITING FOR YOU

The next morning, I was greeted in my bed by Dr. Levi. But Dr. Levi was not alone. As he entered my bedroom, he was followed by my father, who was looking surprisingly dejected, as though his shoulders could not sink lower, and his eyes were trained towards the ground. Then another man in a black suit, dressed just like Dr. Levi, entered. He had the air of some sort of authority, wore wireframe glasses just like Dr. Levi, and was writing something on a small clipboard. Upon seeing me, he finished off his notes and concealed the clipboard in his suit pocket.

Dr. Levi looked expectantly at my dad, who looked in my direction but could not meet my eye. His expression was downcast as he grudgingly spoke. "Ishmael, these men are here to help you, but you need to get up now and follow them. Please."

I looked at my father in alarm, asking with my eyes and being greeted with nothing. My father could not bear to look at me. What was the meaning of this?

I clutched my pillow to my chest. I grabbed my book, as though hoping it would somehow deliver me from this uncomfortable situation. The man in the black suit looked at me from behind his wireframe glasses. Dr. Levi cleared his throat.

"Where's my mom?" I asked defensively.

Dr. Levi gave my father that *look* again, and again my father grimaced slightly, and turned to my direction, his head tilted even more down to the floor, as though the weight was far too great, becoming now unbearable. "She's...waiting for you...outside. You just follow these men, and they'll help you."

I stayed in my bed, looking up at the two formidable men looking down at me, and my father, not looking at me at all, looking at the ground. Then Dr. Levi approached me, a type of grim composure set on his face. He leaned over me and started speaking, sternly. These words, however, brushed by my ears, and I only heard droning as I looked into his cold face and could only see in his cold eyes the cold stone that had my mother's name engraven onto it, flushed with the rain...I must warn my mother...who were these men, trying to take me away? Would they really help me find her, if I just followed them? But Dr. Levi was done speaking, distressed that I had apparently given no attention to his words. I buried my face in my pillow, trying not to think, trying to forget that they were here. Maybe they would just vanish, maybe I was just making them up because I was lonely. Maybe.

After a couple minutes I took my face from my pillow and looked about the room. The two men had gone. My father alone remained, his presence much like a crumpled piece of paper that had been thrown in the corner. So the other two had vanished after all...? But no, I heard their voices murmuring in the hall just outside. Perhaps they thought I could not overhear them, but no matter what they thought, I could hear their words, although the sentences they formed were unclear and disjointed. Some jumbled words that sounded like "sew a side watch" and "safe place" or "safe space." I didn't quite know. But then I heard the words "knife" and "cut" and "arms" and my blood went cold again. So they *were* talking about me. But there was no mention of Berg, of course. I shook my head in sheer disbelief. Then Dr. Levi reappeared with that other man who looked so much like him.

"Come now, Ishmael, please don't be difficult."

"But my mother, is she there?"

"Yes Ishmael. She would like to see you."

"Does she really want to see me?" I asked.

Dr. Levi for the first time looked inexplicably pained. As though he couldn't bear to speak, and yet he spoke, the words coming unwanted from his mouth. "Yes, she does want to see you, Ishmael. Very much."

Epilogue...

As I walk down the grey hall with those formidable suits and black pants, I cannot help but mull over the lunacy Dr. Levi was trying to tell me. Something about my past. Something terrible that happened. I wonder if Mother were here, what she would think. I wonder where she is. I must warn her, tell her of what's coming, try how I can to change the future, to keep it from ever happening to her, to protect her. But something that Dr. Levi said still nags relentlessly at my mind, a crazy thought I cannot afford to accept. Something about my past, something about the flashes of light in my psyche. I'm not sure what I told him about these visions. What I saw, or didn't see. I don't even remember most of these dreams myself. For that matter, I hardly remember real life; anything that happened before we moved to the city. I don't even know exactly why we moved at all. But when I told Dr. Levi about the future, about the funeral, about my mother, about the hospital, and the white blankets, and the graveyard, Dr. Levi told me that these prophetic visions are not glimpses into the future at all.

He said they are memories.

ABOUT THE AUTHOR

Michael Metzler Jr. is an aspiring storyteller from San Diego, California. When not writing poetry and running his baking blog, he's filming music videos and studying film at college.

He currently resides with his family in San Diego County.

This is his first publication.